D0884655

The Famous HONEY BUNCH *Books*

By HELEN LOUISE THORNDYKE

Here is a complete list of these well-loved stories,
in order of publication.

HONEY BUNCH, JUST A LITTLE GIRL
HER FIRST VISIT TO THE CITY
HER FIRST DAYS ON THE FARM
HER FIRST VISIT TO THE SEASHORE
HER FIRST LITTLE GARDEN
HER FIRST DAYS IN CAMP
HER FIRST AUTO TOUR
HER FIRST TRIP ON THE OCEAN
HER FIRST TRIP WEST
HER FIRST SUMMER ON AN ISLAND
HER FIRST TRIP ON THE GREAT LAKES
HER FIRST TRIP IN AN AIRPLANE
HER FIRST VISIT TO THE ZOO
HER FIRST BIG ADVENTURE
HER FIRST BIG PARADE
HER FIRST LITTLE MYSTERY
HER FIRST LITTLE CIRCUS
HER FIRST LITTLE TREASURE HUNT
HER FIRST LITTLE CLUB
HER FIRST TRIP IN A TRAILER
HER FIRST TRIP TO A BIG FAIR
HER FIRST TWIN PLAYMATES
HER FIRST COSTUME PARTY
HER FIRST TRIP ON A HOUSEBOAT
HER FIRST WINTER AT SNOWTOP
HER FIRST TRIP TO THE BIG WOODS
HER FIRST LITTLE PET SHOW
HER FIRST TRIP TO A LIGHTHOUSE
HER FIRST VISIT TO A PONY RANCH
HER FIRST TOUR OF TOY TOWN
HER FIRST VISIT TO PUPPYLAND
HER FIRST TRIP TO REINDEER FARM

"LOOK!" CRIED HONEY BUNCH. "THAT GIRL HAS ON MY DRESS THAT WAS STOLEN!"

Honey Bunch: Her First Little Mystery *Frontispiece (Page 115)*

HONEY BUNCH:
HER FIRST LITTLE MYSTERY

BY

HELEN LOUISE THORNDYKE

NEW YORK
GROSSET & DUNLAP
PUBLISHERS

Printed in the United States of America

Honey Bunch: Her First Little Mystery

CONTENTS

HONEY BUNCH: HER FIRST LITTLE MYSTERY

CHAPTER I

THE MAGIC PROFESSOR

"NOW, Ladies and Gentlemen, if you will be patient for a few minutes," said Norman Clark, making a much better bow than he had ever made in dancing school.

There were no ladies or gentlemen in the living room. There was Honey Bunch, to be sure, but she was not a lady; she was only a little girl. She stood staring at the boy out of great, puzzled blue eyes.

"I'll be very patient, Norman," she promised politely.

The lad frowned.

"My name is Professor Ritz-Carlton, as I've told you twenty times," he scolded. "Did you ever hear of a magic professor called 'Norman'?"

Honey Bunch shook her head. She said she never had.

"But then, I never knew a magic professor before," she explained more cheerfully.

The professor raised his hand. That was the signal for silence. He needed silence when he was about to do a trick, he had told Honey Bunch. Now he set a small glass of water on the table and laid four matches across the top of it.

"Like a little fence," said Honey Bunch, greatly interested.

"Really, Madam," said the Professor with freezing politeness, "really, I must have S-I-L-A-N-C-E."

"Your mother says you're the worst speller in your class," Honey Bunch declared, before she realized she was talking out loud. Then she apologized. "I'm so sorry, Norman, I mean Professor Carlton. I didn't mean to talk."

"You never stop," said the boy bitterly, but he was too much interested in his next trick to quarrel.

He rearranged the matches, then pulled one out. The other three fell into the water.

"See, they float!" he cried, waving his book of directions with one hand and pointing to the glass with the other.

Honey Bunch did not know what she had expected would happen, but she did not think this was very much of a trick. However, she disliked hurting Norman's feelings, so she nodded and smiled.

"Of course, it would be much better if I could have matches that hadn't been burnt," explained Norman. "My mother won't let me have good matches to play with. When my uncle gave me this magic set for my birthday my mother made me promise to use only dead matches."

"It's just as good this way, Norman," Honey Bunch assured him loyally.

"No, it isn't," he argued. "I can't be a real magic professor unless I can do some real tricks. There's one for eggs, only I haven't any eggs. You put three eggs in a hat, and you bring out a chicken. I could do that just as easy if I had the eggs."

Honey Bunch was thrilled. She had once seen a picture of a man taking a live bunny out of a hat, she told Norman.

"We have eggs, Norman, I mean Professor Ritz," she said eagerly. Honey Bunch, it seemed, never could get the professor's whole long name said at one time. "Shall I get you three eggs?"

"Yes, please," Norman beamed. "And say," he called after her, as Honey Bunch started for the kitchen, "get me a hat, will you? Your father's derby hat would be all right."

There was no one in the kitchen, but Honey Bunch knew just where the bowl of eggs stood in the refrigerator. She knew, too, where her daddy's derby hat was — on the shelf in the hall closet. She had to get a chair and stand on it to reach the shelf and even then she wasn't tall enough. But by using her daddy's cane she managed to knock the hat to the floor. It never entered her mind to ask Norman to help her. She thought of him as the "magic professor" who must have everything brought to him so that he could perform his marvelous tricks.

"Those aren't very big eggs," complained Norman, when he saw the three Honey Bunch carried in her father's hat, "but perhaps they'll do."

"Well, I like little chickens best," said Honey Bunch, whose sweet temper did not easily become ruffled. "Make a little chicken come out of the hat, please, Norman. I mean Professor Ritz-Norman."

Norman turned his back to Honey Bunch and read a page in his book. Then he faced her again and bowed three times. This impressed his audience very much.

"I must have silence," the professor warned. "Can I depend upon you not to utter a word, Ladies and Gentlemen?"

"I won't utter," promised Honey Bunch hastily. "I won't utter at all. Will it be a little yellow chicken, Norman?"

"Maybe," said the boy cautiously.

He took the three eggs out of the hat. Then he put them in again. He shook the hat very gently. Honey Bunch watched him intently, but true to her promise she did not say a word. But she jumped when Norman himself began to speak.

"Um-gla!" he cried loudly. "Perla-perla-punka-pump!"

As he spoke he shook the hat up and down.

"Now!" he cried, giving it a final twirl.

"Just take a look at this, will you!"

He held it high above the white goat-skin rug and turned it over. Honey Bunch looked. Out of the hat came not a little yellow chicken, but a stream of yellow liquid that looked remarkably like egg yolks.

"Oh-oh, Norman! Why, Norman Clark!" Honey Bunch was so shocked she forgot to spare the professor's feelings. "Why, Norman Clark, you've broken those eggs! You didn't take a chicken out of the hat at all!"

Norman peered into the hat, as if he thought the chicken might be in there after all.

"I guess I forgot something," he admitted in a very small voice. "I must have left out some of the magic."

"Well,' my gracious, I wish you'd left your-self out, Norman Clark!" came a voice from the doorway, which made both Norman and Honey Bunch jump. "What kind of a mess do you call this? What's that on the rug? Eggs? What are you doing in the living room with eggs? Whose hat is that? Mr. Morton's hat? Stand still. Don't move. You have egg all over your shoes."

Mrs. Miller, the laundress, swept into the room. She was a large woman and usually she was good-natured. But she was not at all pleased to find broken eggs all over the white fur rug and she said that Honey Bunch's mother would not be pleased, either.

"And that good derby hat ruined!" cried Mrs. Miller, picking it up as if she thought it might go off like a firecracker in her hand. "Why don't you take your own hat, Norman Clark, if you want to ruin one?"

Norman explained, very meekly, that he had not meant to ruin any hat. He was performing magic, he said.

"Magic!" Mrs. Miller sniffed. "Well, you stand where you are till I get a basin of water and a cloth. It's a good thing I came in when I did. Something told me you two were up to mischief and I left my wash on the line to come in and look after you. Lucky I did. Another half hour, and you and your magic would have wrecked the house."

When Mrs. Miller bustled in again a few moments later with a basin of cold water and a large cloth and set to work on the rug and Norman's shoes, which had received most of the egg, Honey Bunch asked her a question.

"What told you to come in, Mrs. Miller?" she asked curiously. "You said something told you."

Norman, afraid to move, suggested meekly that maybe it was magic.

"It was my bones," Mrs. Miller declared, scrubbing away vigorously. "I felt in my bones that something was wrong. My bones are worth more to me than all the magic I've ever heard tell of."

This was too much for Norman.

"Maybe you never saw the kind of magic I make," he boasted. "I can do wonderful magic, can't I, Honey Bunch? Shall I show you a trick, Mrs. Miller? A magic trick, out of my book?"

"Can you clean up this rug and this hat?" asked Mrs. Miller, pointing to the derby from which eggs still dripped. "If you can make them as good as new, I'll believe in your magic, Norman Clark."

Alas, that was beyond the boy's powers, as he sadly admitted. So Mrs. Miller cleaned his shoes thoroughly and rolled up the rug to be sent away to the cleaner's and took the derby hat out to the kitchen until she could decide whether it was worth saving. When she had done all these things, she said that Honey Bunch and Norman must come out into the back yard with her.

"I must take in the wash, and it isn't safe to leave you two in the house, it seems," Mrs. Miller declared. "Now that Norman has magic on the brain, how do I know he won't think he is a canary bird and try to fly?"

"I guess you don't understand magic very well, Mrs. Miller," said Norman with dignity.

The laundress laughed. She was really kind-hearted, and Honey Bunch loved her. What the house would have been without Mrs. Miller to wash, and iron, and clean, and sweep, and cook, and bake on the days when Honey Bunch's mother was away, no one knew. Mrs. Miller was always ready to be of help, and she had known Honey Bunch since she was a baby. Norman Clark liked Mrs. Miller, too, though sometimes she did scold him.

The two children followed the stout washerwoman out into the pretty, sunny back yard.

Honey Bunch, who was ahead of Norman, heard Mrs. Miller gasp.

"I never! Who's playing tricks now?" Mrs. Miller stood staring about her.

Honey Bunch pulled at the woman's apron. "What's the matter? Where are the tricks?"

"The clothes-basket!" cried Mrs. Miller, all of a sudden. "It's gone! And three-quarters of the wash in it. All my starched pieces were dry and I had taken them down."

Honey Bunch and Norman stared at the clotheslines. There were several garments hanging on one of the lines and a long row of stockings dangled in the breeze. But there was certainly no clothes-basket anywhere in the garden.

"Is it your magic, Norman?" asked Honey Bunch, much puzzled. "Did you make the basket van-vanish?"

Norman saw Mrs. Miller looking at him. He would have liked to pretend that his "magic" had caused the clothes to disappear, but he decided that Mrs. Miller would not take kindly to any such make-believe.

"I didn't even see the clothes-basket," he protested.

"No, you didn't—you were in the house," said Mrs. Miller kindly.

From the back yard they could look through the side yard to the street. Now two little girls called "Hello!" cheerily.

"Oh-oh, Ida! Grace!" Honey Bunch beckoned importantly to her friends. "Come here, quick! Guess what happened!"

Ida Camp and Grace Winters came dashing through the yard, eager to hear the news.

"The clothes-basket—" began Honey Bunch, but Norman could not wait for her to finish.

"It's gone!" cried Norman.

Ida and Grace stared. How could they guess what Honey Bunch and Norman meant?

"When I was in the house, my clothes-basket with the wash in it disappeared," explained Mrs. Miller more calmly.

"But where is it?" asked Grace, who had never heard of a clothes-basket disappearing before.

Ida, who was the best friend of Honey Bunch and a very sensible, quiet little girl, suggested that they had better search the yard.

"Maybe you put it down somewhere and forgot it, Mrs. Miller," said Ida. "My mother sometimes forgets where she puts things."

Mrs. Miller declared that there was nothing wrong with her memory, but she agreed it might be a good plan to look around. She and the four children hunted behind the bushes and even up on the back porch. Norman Clark obligingly climbed to the top of the fence and looked into his own yard—he lived back of Honey Bunch. But no one could find the missing clothes-basket.

"Now, if your magic were any good, Norman," said Mrs. Miller rather crossly, for she was tired and worried, "you would be able to wave your stick and produce that basket. You could make it come up out of the grass."

Honey Bunch didn't hear this. She was darting down the side yard toward the street.

"Where are you going?" Mrs. Miller called after the little girl. Perhaps she was afraid Honey Bunch, like the clothes-basket, might disappear too.

"I see a policeman!" Honey Bunch cried, without stopping. "I'm going to tell him our wash is lost!"

CHAPTER II

WHO STOLE THE BASKET?

THE policeman, who was very tall and slim, was standing with his stick under his arm, gazing intently up the street. Honey Bunch tugged at his coat.

"Oh, please, do you think you could find our wash?" she begged, giving the bluecoat a pull for every word.

When the policeman turned and saw the little girl, he smiled. He was young and pleasant-looking, and Honey Bunch later told Mrs. Miller that she didn't believe he would scold even a burglar.

"Anything wrong?" asked the policeman, bending down so he could hear better what Honey Bunch had to say. "Lost your ball down the sewer basin again?"

"I never drop my ball down the sewer!" Honey Bunch informed him indignantly. "It's our wash. It's lost."

"Well, you shouldn't leave it on the street,"

said the policeman gravely. "Maybe the wind blew it away."

"No, it was when Norman was making magic," Honey Bunch declared, talking as loudly as she could, for she felt she must make the policeman understand. "He was doing magic with eggs in a hat, and someone took the clothes-basket. It's gone."

"Where," said the policeman, "are the eggs?"

"They broke, and Mrs. Miller wiped them up, and the rug has to go to the cleaner's." Honey Bunch took another breath. "My daddy's derby hat is all eggy and the starched pieces are in the basket. Mrs. Miller felt it in her bones."

The policeman laughed and patted Honey Bunch on her head.

"Take it easy, take it easy," he advised. "You'd better think it over and let me know whether you've lost a clothes-basket or an omelet."

Honey Bunch didn't know what to do next. She saw that the policeman was laughing at her. Perhaps he did not believe her at all. Surely a policeman ought to know how to find missing clothes-baskets. People always told policemen about lost things. Honey Bunch remembered when she had found a lost baby, and her daddy and mother had told them about that right away.

You may know about this lost baby Honey Bunch found. Indeed, if you have read the book just before this one, called "Honey Bunch: Her First Big Parade," then you do know all about the baby Honey Bunch called Dolly, and who was so small that Norman Clark thought she couldn't speak English when she talked baby words.

It is likely, too, that you have read the other books about Honey Bunch, which tell of her visits and her travels; how she made a prize garden; her adventures on her first automobile tour; her first airplane trip. You know, if you've read these stories, that this little girl's real name is Gertrude Marion Morton, and that her daddy was the first to call her "Honey Bunch," because he said that name suited her better than her real one. You probably remember Mrs. Miller, and Lady Clare, Honey Bunch's beautiful pussy cat, and about Norman Clark, and many other neighborhood friends of this dear little girl.

But this is not helping Honey Bunch out of her present troubles, is it? We really do not know what she would have done if Mrs. Miller had not come bustling up, all out of breath, with Norman and Ida and Grace close behind her.

"Have you seen a thief?" asked the laundress, who was red in the face from running.

"No, nor a clothes-basket," the policeman assured her. "Nor an omelet," he added.

"Now, young man, don't try to be funny," Mrs. Miller scolded, smoothing down her hair on top. "My second-best clothes-basket, with two-thirds of a good wash in it, has disappeared. A clothes-basket doesn't walk off on its own legs, does it, if it hasn't any legs?"

The policeman stopped laughing. He pulled out a little notebook and a pencil.

"Is this your residence, Madam?" he asked, glancing up at the number of the house.

Honey Bunch, Ida, Grace and Norman pressed closer to listen.

"Mercy no, I don't live here," said Mrs. Miller. "I do day's work and laundry. I'm staying here the better part of the week while

Mr. and Mrs. Morton are away on a business trip. This is their house—Mr. David Morton's house. And a fine thing it will be, if they come home and find the best linen napkins, not to mention a pair of Mr. Morton's silk pajamas, gone."

The policeman asked several questions. When did the basket disappear? Had the wash ever been missing before? Had anyone else on the block lost their laundry recently?

"I'd like to have a list of the clothes that are missing too," he said, writing busily in his little book. "Describe them briefly, please."

Mrs. Miller sighed. She remembered the napkins, she said—eight of them with monograms. And the gray silk pajamas. But how could she remember all the other things?

"There were some of my dresses, Mrs. Miller," Honey Bunch reminded her. "My green bloomer dress and the plaid one."

"There was a sheet," Norman chimed in, "because I stepped on it by mistake when you were just starting to hang out the clothes."

"A sheet!" Mrs. Miller frowned at him. "I'll have you know there were seven sheets, eight pillow slips, and at least a dozen towels. Oh, yes, and a pink and blue checked dress for a little girl."

"Oh-oh!" wailed Honey Bunch. "That was my favorite dress. My Aunt Carol sent it to me. I didn't know that was in the basket, too."

The policeman snapped a rubber band around his book which he put into his pocket.

"I'll make a report," he said, "and I'll be around in the morning to see if anything has developed. Looks like a case of a passing thief to me. I'll take a look around your yard."

Everyone helped the policeman. He went into the laundry, too. The children got in his way, but he did not seem to mind that. They told him their names and he told them his. He was Peter Noble. He said he had not been a policeman very long, for he was only twenty-three years old.

When he started to go back to the police station Norman Clark wanted to go with him, but Peter Noble said he thought it would be better if Norman were to stay home and practice his magic.

"Try to get that checked dress back for the

little girl with the blue eyes," Peter Noble suggested, smiling at Honey Bunch.

After he had gone Mrs. Miller set to work to take in the clothes that were left on the lines, whether they were dry or not. She said for all she knew they might disappear even if there was no clothes-basket in which to carry them off.

The children sat down on the back steps to talk of the "robbery," as Ida Camp called it, and Honey Bunch admitted that she was almost ready to cry.

"My pink and blue checked dress was my prettiest one," she declared. "It was almost new. It had a white piqué collar and cuffs and white buttons. I've worn it only five times."

Then a very determined look came into her blue eyes.

"I'll find the mean people who took my prettiest dress!" she declared, so fiercely that Norman looked startled. "I'll find them and make them give it back to me."

"We'll help you, Honey Bunch!" Ida Camp promised. "We'll all help you. Say, we can form a detective club. I saw one in the movies. The policemen can't find out anything, but a lot of people follow clues and solve mysteries. We can tell one another when we find a clue—it will be lots of fun."

"I'll be the chief detector!" cried Norman Clark.

"I guess you won't!" Ida was usually gentle, but she and Norman never got along very well together. "Honey Bunch is head detector, because it's her clothes-basket we have to trace. I'll be the second, Grace can be the third detector, and you can be the fourth, if you like."

Norman argued that he ought to be "head detector" because he was a boy, but Ida told him he couldn't belong to the club at all, unless he was willing to do as she said. So, rather than be left out of everything, Norman agreed to regard Honey Bunch as the chief detective.

"I don't promise not to work my magic," he warned the girls. "I'll experiment by myself, and when I make a great discovery don't expect me to tell you about it. I'll probably capture the thief all by myself."

He was so intent on the idea of making his

magic help him that he hurried into Honey Bunch's house to get his box and his wand and the old white leather gloves his mother had given him to wear when he was a magician.

Mrs. Miller had come out into the yard again and was talking across the fence to Mrs. Clark. Honey Bunch knew that the laundress must be telling Norman's mother about the missing clothes-basket, but she was surprised to have Mrs. Miller stop at the steps, instead of going down into the laundry after she and Mrs. Clark had finished their talk.

"Mrs. Clark told me a funny thing, Honey Bunch," said the woman slowly. "When I was telling her about our missing clothes-basket just now, she said she'd seen Jake Silberman carrying a basket of something past her house an hour or so ago."

Honey Bunch stared. Ida Camp gasped. Grace Winters murmured "My goodness!" Each of them was sure that Jake Silberman had been carrying the clothes-basket.

"Mrs. Clark didn't say it was a clothes-basket and she didn't say it wasn't," Mrs. Miller admitted when the children questioned her. "She said she was sewing at her front window and happened to look out, and there he was carrying a basket of something. She couldn't see what it was."

Mrs. Miller went down into the laundry and the three little girls stood up.

"Let's go to Jake Silberman's!" said Honey Bunch in a mysterious whisper.

"It isn't very far," Ida whispered.

"Don't tell Norman," said Grace, and with that they all scurried out of the yard, lest the boy should come out of the house and insist upon going with them.

All the girls knew Jake Silberman. Every child in the neighborhood did. He was a little, bent old man with a gray beard, and bought and sold second-hand things, such as furniture, clothes, and even automobiles. He lived in a shabby house which was surrounded on three sides by a large yard. It was rumored that he chased any children he found in this garden. But, as Honey Bunch pointed out, perhaps he would not chase them if they did not run.

"Perhaps he won't be at home," said Ida Camp, half hoping he would be away.

CHAPTER III

THE SEARCH

JAKE SILBERMAN'S house wasn't very far from Honey Bunch's house, but the three little girls made the walk longer than it really was, because they went around some of the blocks twice. This was Ida's idea. She said that if Norman happened to be following them, he would think they were merely taking a walk and not going to any special place.

Honey Bunch had often seen the Silberman house, but she had never looked at it very carefully. When they finally reached it, Honey Bunch saw that though the yard had a fence around it, there was no gate. There was a gap in the fence, though, which was large enough for an automobile or a wagon to drive through.

"I shouldn't think Mrs. Silberman would like her front lawn to look so messy," sniffed Grace Winters disapprovingly. "My mother would send us out to pick up things, if our place looked like this."

Honey Bunch and Ida agreed that the spot did look "messy." The house was pleasant enough to look at, though it needed painting. There were clean white curtains at the windows and some green bushes around the door. But the yard! There was almost no grass, only a few worn patches here and there. A huge pile of old iron, which filled one corner, made a sort of tower. Honey Bunch wondered why it did not topple over. In another corner were some broken-down automobiles without wheels, and several wheels without any cars on them. Rocking chairs without any seats in them rocked lonesomely on the ground. It was very messy, indeed, but to the three little girls peering at it it was also very fascinating.

"Let's go inside," said Honey Bunch, who was sure that she saw everything in the world in that yard *except* a clothes-basket.

The three, keeping hold of hands, walked through the gap in the fence. They were not interested in the old automobiles, nor in the tangled mass of furniture. As Grace Winters remarked, they could see old tables and chairs and sofas at home any time.

"My mother likes antics," said Ida suddenly. "Maybe we can find some antics while we're looking for the clothes-basket Jake Silberman stole."

"Maybe he didn't steal it," Honey Bunch protested.

"What's an antic?" demanded Grace.

"It's a piece of old furniture," Ida explained. "But it has to be the right kind. It's nicer if it belonged to George Washington or to some king. Kings had lots ot antics in their houses."

Honey Bunch said that kings lived in castles. Ida admitted that she had meant to say castles. However, Ida added, she did not see anything that looked like an "antic" in the yard.

"We haven't looked all over yet," said Honey Bunch, who was a persevering little girl. "Let's peek in that corner—there's a pile of things we haven't seen."

The pile did not look very inviting at first. Three or four old wash tubs, some boxes and a bench or two had been carelessly tossed together in a heap. A little apart from the things was an old trunk. The girls did not pay any attention to it because Ida insisted they must help her turn over the wash tubs.

"If Jake has wash tubs, he might want the clothes-basket, don't you see?" argued Ida. "Maybe his wife didn't have a clothes-basket. Help me turn over these tubs—I'll bet Mrs. Miller's basket and the wash are under one of them."

Honey Bunch and Ida and Grace tugged, and finally did succeed in overturning one of the heavy wooden tubs. Grace screamed when some tiny black bugs began to scurry about, but Honey Bunch seized her by the arm.

"Lo-ok!" stammered Honey Bunch. "Oh-oh, look, quick!"

She pointed toward the trunk, and Ida and Grace stared.

"It's moving!" Ida gasped. "Come away, quick. The trunk's moving."

Sure enough, the trunk was moving. That is, it gave little hops and jerks. For a moment it would be perfectly still, then it would give a jump. Ida kept pulling at Honey Bunch's sleeve, begging her to run.

"I'm not going," said Honey Bunch firmly, though her voice shook. "I'm not going until I find out what's in the trunk."

This was too much, even for Grace.

"Why, Honey Bunch, are you crazy?" she cried. "Don't go near that dreadful trunk. Come on, we're going home. Aren't we going home, Ida?"

Poor Ida was scared, but she was loyal, too.

"I won't go without Honey Bunch," she said. "Oh, please, Honey Bunch, won't you come before something catches us?"

Honey Bunch took a step toward the trunk. She was afraid, too, but meant to find out what was making the trunk behave so queerly.

"There couldn't be anything in it," she argued. "You know there couldn't be anything in a trunk, Ida."

"Oh, there couldn't?" asked Grace, speaking before Ida could say a word. "Well, I guess if a lion or a tiger or—or an elephant jumps out of that trunk, Honey Bunch Morton, you'll wish you hadn't been so silly. I'm going." Then Grace actually did go—as far as the fence, where she stood looking back to see what might happen next.

Honey Bunch began to tiptoe toward the trunk. Ida, who would not leave her playmate, began to tiptoe too. The trunk gave a little hop.

"I'll just lift the lid and then get ready to run," whispered Honey Bunch. "Don't stand too close, Ida, or I might knock you over when I start."

As Grace watched, Honey Bunch and Ida reached the trunk. It was still, now. Ida stepped to one side. Honey Bunch took hold of the lid. It did not open easily, and she forgot to be afraid as she tugged at it. As she gave it an extra hard pull, it flew up.

Then Honey Bunch said "Land sakes!" That was what Mrs. Miller often said when she was surprised.

"Well, I never!" cried Ida, who was surprised, too.

"What is it?" called Grace. "What did you find?"

"Don't tell her—make her come and see," urged Ida.

Honey Bunch did not answer, for she was busy trying to get a rather plump, small boy out of a small space. Norman Clark had wedged himself so tightly in the trunk that he could not get out quickly. His face was red, and he breathed fast as the little girl clutched him.

"Ow! You pinch me! Let me alone—I can get myself out," cried Norman, making the trunk rock in earnest as he twisted and turned.

"You will scare me, will you!" Honey Bunch scolded, pulling at his blouse. "You think you're funny, don't you, Norman Clark!" She gave a final tug, and the boy fell out of the trunk. There was a crackling sound as he landed on his elbows and lay, half of him on the ground, the other half in the lid of the trunk.

"Ho, it was nothing but Norman Clark!" said Grace Winters, who had gained enough courage to come back. "That's all it was—just Norman Clark."

The lad crawled out all the way and turned to see Honey Bunch trying to crawl in where he had been.

"What are you trying to do?" protested Norman. "You'll get stuck in there, same as I did."

Honey Bunch stood up. Her face was

flushed and her hair was in her eyes, but she shook it straight.

"Look!" she said.

She held out her hand, palm up. On it lay a string of pearls.

"I found it in the trunk!" cried Honey Bunch. "It was wrapped in a piece of paper —see."

She leaned over and brought up a small piece of paper from the bottom of the trunk. It had once been white, but now was a yellow-brown, and so thin and old that it was cracked in a dozen places.

"The beads fell out of there," explained Honey Bunch, pointing to a tiny hole in one corner of the folded paper.

"I didn't see any beads!" objected Norman, who seemed to feel cheated. "I looked at the trunk before I got in it and I didn't see any beads."

"They fell out of a pocket—here it is." The four children bent over the trunk while Honey Bunch pointed out a rip in the faded and stained lining. Behind this was a tiny drawer, hardly any bigger than a little pill box. No one would ever have known it was there, if the lining had remained pasted over it.

"There's writing on the paper," said Honey Bunch, making a new discovery as she turned it over. "Look, there's writing in ink. Maybe it says something about the beads."

Norman Clark was supposed to be the best reader in the group and he took the paper, sure that he could tell what were the words written on it.

"Well, the ink's very poor," he complained, as if that was Honey Bunch's fault. "The ink's very poor, and I think something's been spilled on the paper."

Then Grace Winters tried to read it, but she said she thought it was written in Latin.

"When you see words written in that little tiny handwriting it's almost always Latin," said Grace, who had a cousin who was a high school teacher.

"I think we ought to look in the trunk for more things," said Ida, who could not read even print very well and did not want to try this paper. "Come on, let's look in the trunk again. Maybe we can find some more things."

Whatever else there might be, the children

were not to discover, for at that moment a loud coughing and choking sound was heard, and into the yard there rolled a battered car. At the wheel sat a short, bent, fat man with a gray beard. In the back of the auto was a lot of old furniture and on top of the furniture were three worn tires.

"It's Silberman!" whispered Norman. "We'd better duck."

But the second-hand dealer had seen them, and began to shout.

"Here, you, what you doing in my yard! Wait till I catch you! I'll teach you to come snooping around my place, stealing my things. I'll teach you."

The car was between the children and the opening in the fence, and they wondered how they could get out. But Jake Silberman was fat and he was not young. He had not done much running for years and years. So, though he leaped down and came tearing across the ground, the children managed to dodge him. Honey Bunch and Ida darted one way, Norman and Grace ran another.

The piles of old stuff in the yard helped them, because they could run behind the junk.

Jake Silberman only wasted his breath in shouting and waving his arms. Of course, he could not run two ways at once, so in a minute Honey Bunch and Ida dashed through the open space.

They would not run away and leave Norman and Grace, so they waited while these two youngsters ran around the old automobiles and dashed behind the towering pile of iron, before they could escape. In a few minutes all four children found themselves safe in the street, rushing pell-mell for home.

"He'll know we were looking in the trunk!" gasped Honey Bunch as they went along, "because we left the lid open."

"Who cares?" Ida cried, almost out of breath. "Don't lose the pretty pearl beads, Honey Bunch!"

CHAPTER IV

THE POLICEMAN

THE children did not stop running until they reached Honey Bunch's house. Mrs. Miller, who was accustomed to being in charge of the Morton home whenever Mr. and Mrs. Morton were away, looked up as the three little girls and Norman burst into her kitchen, demanding drinks of water.

"How you do tear around!" she reproved. "Honey Bunch, I wish you wouldn't go off without letting me know about it. And Norman, your mother has been hunting for you. She wants you to help her."

The boy went home so willingly that Mrs. Miller asked Honey Bunch if she thought he was sick. "I never saw that child leave here without being pulled away," the laundress said.

Honey Bunch suspected that Norman would feel safer in his own house in case Jake Silberman should come after him. But she did not say this. Instead, she explained to Mrs. Miller that the reason why she had not said she was going out was that Norman was not supposed to know where the girls were.

"We thought he was in the house collecting his magic set," Honey Bunch declared. "If I had come in to tell you I was going, I thought he might hear me and want to be with us. But he must have heard us talking through the window, because he got there first."

Mrs. Miller was very busy now, ironing the clothes which were left, and going to the front door to look up and down the street in the hope that someone might be bringing back the basket to her, so she did not ask where "there" might be. Honey Bunch's mother would have asked, but Mrs. Miller was too worried about the lost clothes.

Honey Bunch, Ida and Grace went upstairs to the playroom. Then they had their first real chance to look at the pearl beads, which were of a beautiful, faintly rosy color, twenty-four in number. Honey Bunch said they were the prettiest she had ever seen.

"I like the clasp," Ida declared, fingering

it gently. "It's just thick with rhinestones. We never had as good a clasp as this one for our beads, did we?"

Honey Bunch and Ida and Grace had often strung beads for their best and biggest dolls. Sometimes they just knotted the thread and slipped the necklaces over the heads of the dolls. When someone gave them an old necklace with a clasp, they could make very elegant bead chains indeed. But, as Honey Bunch had once complained, hardly anyone would give away a chain of beads with a *good* clasp. Usually one half of it would be broken. They could not remember ever having had a clasp that twinkled as this one did.

"We ought to scrub it well and make it shine," said Grace Winters critically. "There's lots of dirt in between the stones."

Grace was famous for liking to wash things. Her mother said she took the enamel right off her dolls' faces, and she actually did scrub the stone out of the setting in her birthday ring. Honey Bunch did not want her friend to wash all the rhinestones out of this pretty clasp.

"Let's wait till my mother comes home,"

she suggested tactfully. "She knows how to clean jewelry. She has pink sawdust and little brushes and everything. Hilda can wear the beads till my mother gets back."

Hilda was Honey Bunch's largest doll. She was as large as a real baby two years old would be. Indeed, when Dolly, the little lost baby, had lived with Honey Bunch, she had worn Hilda's clothes. Honey Bunch fastened the pearl beads around Hilda's neck now and they hung down a little on the lace yoke of her dress.

"What are you going to do with the paper?" asked Grace.

Before Honey Bunch could answer, Mrs. Miller called that Ida's mother had telephoned. She wanted Ida to come home and Grace was to come with her.

"We have to practice a duet," explained Grace, who thought that being a detective was much more interesting than being a musician.

Honey Bunch, left alone, sat down to think. She was trying to remember what she had done with the paper around the pearl beads. She stayed in the playroom so long, that good Mrs. Miller climbed the stairs, even though she had a leg that bothered her "off and on," as she said, to see if anything was wrong.

"Every time I see that doll she reminds me of Dolly," Mrs. Miller exclaimed, glancing at Hilda, who sat smiling in her own little rocking chair. "I do wish you'd come downstairs, Honey Bunch," the woman went on, "and play in the yard a while. I want to put some napkins on the grass to bleach and I don't dare leave them there with no one to watch them. Your mother wouldn't like it if she should come home and find her best set of lunch napkins stolen."

Mrs. Miller could talk of nothing except the missing clothes-basket and the wash in it all the rest of the afternoon. After supper she kept on till Honey Bunch went to bed. The laundress explained that she felt responsible for everything, because Honey Bunch's daddy had left her in charge of the house.

"I'd have more faith in that policeman finding out something," said Mrs. Miller, "if he wasn't so young. He probably hasn't got his mind on robbers at all."

"Can he take his mind off and on robbers?" asked Honey Bunch, remembering what Mrs.

Miller said about her leg that sometimes hurt.

"I think he takes it mostly off," Mrs. Miller said. Then she saw the clock and said it was high time that Honey Bunch was asleep.

In the morning the first thing the little girl heard was the sound of rain. And the first thing Mrs. Miller said, when she came in to see if Honey Bunch needed any help with her dressing was, "I suppose those clothes will be covered with mud if we ever get them back."

Honey Bunch did not mind a rainy day. She had her breakfast, and then, when Mrs. Miller announced she was going to clean the silver, Honey Bunch decided to do some clay modeling at the other end of the kitchen table. They were both working very hard, when someone knocked at the kitchen door.

"Let *me* go!" cried Honey Bunch, scrambling down from her high stool. "Maybe it's Luke."

Luke was the grocery boy, and he was a great friend of Honey Bunch. However, it was not Luke this time. When the little girl opened the kitchen door, there on the back porch stood a tall, slim figure in a dark slicker and high boots.

"It's Peter Noble!" the delighted Honey Bunch shouted. "Look, Mrs. Miller, here's Peter Noble. He has his mind on robbers—you said he mostly takes it off, you know."

Mrs. Miller blushed a deep red, and the man began to laugh. Though he did not understand what Honey Bunch meant, he suspected that the laundress did not have much faith in his ability as a policeman.

"Good morning, Mrs. Miller," he said politely. "It's a shame to mark up your beautiful clean floor."

"You can't hurt good linoleum," Mrs. Miller replied. "Do come in. Have you had your breakfast? Where's your umbrella?"

Peter Noble said he had had his breakfast and that he never carried an umbrella. He came into the kitchen and closed the door.

"Sit down, do," Mrs. Miller hospitably urged him. "I don't suppose you brought back my clothes-basket and the wash?"

The woman looked a little disappointed when the policeman said "No." Perhaps she thought he had left it on the porch and meant to surprise her.

"As a matter of fact," the young man said, "we seem to be exactly where we were. Not a single clue to work on yet. Of course, it's a new case, and we need a little time."

Mrs. Miller sniffed and began to polish a teaspoon. Honey Bunch was afraid the sniff might hurt the policeman's feelings. The little girl wondered if she ought to tell him of the "clue" she and Ida and Grace had followed. No, she decided to herself, she would not do that. She ought not to tell anyone without first asking Ida and Grace. Besides, it was their clue and perhaps they might find the wash all by themselves and surprise the police department.

But if Mrs. Miller did sniff, she meant no unkindness by it. She brought out a plate of her nicest cinnamon star cookies and told Peter Noble to help himself.

"Thanks," he said, as he took a very large bite. "Say, these are good cookies!" he cried, very much as Norman Clark might have put it. "You know," continued the policeman, "I remember we had a funny case a year or two ago in which cookies figured. A woman lost her diamond ring. Said she left it on the kitchen table and then accused the grocery boy of taking it."

"Luke wouldn't steal anything!" cried Honey Bunch indignantly. "Would he, Mrs. Miller?"

"Well, this lad's name was Cornelius, 'Corny' for short," the policeman explained. "The woman made a terrible fuss about her ring and it looked bad for Corny. One night she had some friends come in to listen to the radio and passed them a plate of cookies. In one of them was her diamond ring, baked right in. The ring had melted, but the diamond was all right."

Honey Bunch stared, round-eyed, and Mrs. Miller tapped a fork on the table to attract her attention.

"Listen to me, Honey Bunch Morton!" said Mrs. Miller very earnestly. "There aren't any diamond rings in the cookies I bake. If you're a good cook you notice what's going on about you. That woman couldn't have had her mind on her baking."

"Tell some more," begged Honey Bunch. She thought how interested Norman would be if he could hear a real, live policeman talking like this.

"Well, people do funny things," Peter Noble said thoughtfully, beginning on another cookie. "We had an old lady come in, all upset because her maid had sold her muff to a ragman. The old lady told us she had one thousand dollars sewn into the lining of that muff. We upset the city for a week, hunting for the ragman. When we found him he proved that what the maid had sold him was an old fur laprobe and there wasn't a nickel in the lining. Then the old lady recollected that she had put the muff in fur storage the winter before."

Mrs. Miller laughed and said *that* came from having more things to take care of than one could look after.

"I go through my attic twice a year and clear it out," she said proudly. "I don't keep antiques, the way lots of people do."

Honey Bunch almost bit her tongue. So Ida had meant to say "antiques" when she talked about "antics." Honey Bunch made up her mind to tell Ida about this word some day when they were by themselves.

"My mother's the one to save things," announced the policeman, biting into his sixth cookie. "She hates to part with her old things. As a matter of fact, we had something stolen from our attic when I was a lad that changed my whole life. My family intended that I should be a doctor, and here I am a policeman."

"Who stole what?" asked Honey Bunch, much excited.

"Oh, a bunch of heirlooms," the policeman answered. "Things that had been my great-grandmother's and some that had been her mother's. My mother set great store by these things. We were living in a house that had belonged to my great-grandmother and the attic was heaped with valuable stuff. I remember my mother saying there was a set of sables and a collection of laces, old books and miniatures painted on ivory, and some valuable jewelry. The loss made my mother almost ill, for none of those things could ever be replaced. We had the house overrun with police and detectives for weeks, and I talked to them all. We have never recovered any of the valuables, but when I finished school I announced I meant to join the Police Force. And here I am."

"I'd like to be a policeman, too," announced Honey Bunch hopefully.

"Thank goodness, that's one thing a girl can't be," Mrs. Miller replied, screwing down the lid on the silver polish box, for she had finished cleaning.

"Well, she might be a policewoman," said Peter Noble, with a teasing smile. He liked to provoke good Mrs. Miller.

Honey Bunch at once had half a dozen questions to ask about policewomen. What kind of uniforms did they wear? What did they do? Did they have pistols? Could they direct traffic? Could Ida Camp be a policewoman, too?

The young man answered these questions as well as he could, but finally had to suggest that Honey Bunch wait a few years, because, he said, the styles in policewomen might change.

"What's that?" cried Mrs. Miller, jumping as a curious tap sounded at the door.

Tap-tap, it sounded again.

"Shall I go?" asked the policeman. It was

not his house, you see, and he did not know what Mrs. Miller might want him to do.

Tap-tap-tap came the queer noise at the door.

"I know what it is!" cried Honey Bunch, clapping her hands. "I'll bet I know what it is. Want me to tell you, Mrs. Miller?"

CHAPTER V

A DOG IN TROUBLE

"DON'T go near that door!" Mrs. Miller told Honey Bunch. "Keep away! I'll see who's there."

"It's magic," said Honey Bunch wisely. "I think that's what it is, Mrs. Miller. Norman is making magic and the magic is bringing back our clothes-basket."

The laundress looked puzzled. She did not believe in magic, and she especially did not believe in any magic Norman Clark might produce.

"Tap-tap!" sounded the odd noise again.

"Well, all right—" Mrs. Miller nodded to Honey Bunch, who ran to the door and opened it wide.

Something small and white dashed in. Then up rose Lady Clare, the beautiful black cat, who had been asleep under the gas range.

"Down, Hunter!" cried Peter sternly. "Down, I say!"

Honey Bunch called to her cat not to be afraid, but neither cat nor dog heard a word. Lady Clare dashed for the living room, Hunter raced after her, and behind them ran Mrs. Miller, Honey Bunch and the policeman.

Lady Clare had never been chased by an impudent fox-terrier right in her own house, and she was so astonished she did not know what to do. As it happened, she did the worst possible thing, which was to leap to the top of a floor lamp. Perhaps she thought that was almost as good as a tree, but it was not, for a tree has roots in the ground and cannot easily be toppled over.

Before Peter Noble could reach out to catch the floor lamp it had swayed and fallen. The rose-colored silk shade fell in one direction, with Lady Clare clinging to it, and the heavy metal base of the lamp crashed in the direction of Mrs. Miller. It struck her, and she groaned as if it had hurt her. Lady Clare dashed upstairs, and they could hear the dog barking madly as he followed her.

"Young man, you go get your dog!" commanded Mrs. Miller. "Never mind me, I'm

LADY CLARE HAD NEVER BEEN CHASED BY AN IMPUDENT FOX-TERRIER RIGHT IN HER OWN HOUSE.

Honey Bunch: Her First Little Mystery Page 48

all right. But a cat and dog, let loose in a house, can do a lot of damage."

The policeman only waited to set the lamp upright. Then he ran for the stairs. After him whirled Honey Bunch, eager to rescue her pet.

Hunter was a small, sleek fox-terrior, not much bigger than Lady Clare. So, wherever she went, he could follow. They had already whirled themselves in and out of the guest room, when Honey Bunch and Peter Noble reached the second floor.

"They're in Mother's room!" cried Honey Bunch, hearing a great snarling and spitting across the hall. "Oh, Mr. Noble, don't let Hunter hurt Lady Clare."

As she said that, something crashed, and out of Mrs. Morton's room shot a ruffled, fiery-eyed black cat. After her galloped a white dog with brown spots. Hunter's tongue was hanging out and he was having such an exciting time that he never once heard his master calling to him to behave himself.

Honey Bunch peered into her mother's room. One set of drapes at the side window had been torn down. Probably Lady Clare had tried to climb up the curtains and had pulled down the light brass fixtures.

"Is there another floor?" asked Peter Noble, glancing around for the stairway.

For answer, Honey Bunch dashed ahead of him and led the way up to the third floor. To her relief, the playroom door was closed, but a tinkle of broken glass, followed by an angry "Meow!" together with several short, loud barks, told the searchers that Lady Clare and Hunter were into more mischief.

"They're in the storeroom!" cried Honey Bunch. "Oh! they must be knocking over something."

An object fell to the floor with a crash and more broken glass tinkled. The policeman ran down the hall and reached the storeroom door just as Lady Clare, hissing and spitting, sped out and made for the stairs.

Hunter was close at her heels, but Peter Noble was too quick for him. The young man closed the door in such haste that he nipped Hunter, at which that surprised animal yelped.

"Well, it serves you right!" his master scolded. "Why don't you behave yourself in a strange house? It's bad enough to have you follow me, without scaring a cat into fits, knocking over lamps, and breaking all the perfume bottles, isn't it?"

Honey Bunch patted the little dog's head, and he wagged his tail doubtfully. He was so tired that when the policeman scooped him up he lay quiet in the man's arms, panting.

"Don't scold him," begged Honey Bunch. "My daddy says dogs just have to chase cats, that they can't help it. And all the glass we heard is pickle bottles — Mrs. Miller keeps lots of old pickle bottles on shelves in the storeroom. I'm glad Hunter didn't get into the playroom, though, for my best doll Hilda is in there and she's dressed up in one of her good dresses and a string of——"

Honey Bunch stopped just in time. She did not mean to tell Peter Noble about the pearl beads. Ida and Grace might not like that. After all, the policeman did not belong to the Detective Club.

Peter Noble did not notice that Honey Bunch had not finished her sentence. He was afraid he might be late in reporting to his precinct station, so he hurried downstairs, carrying Hunter to make sure that the little dog did not do any more hunting around in that house.

"I'm awfully sorry, Mrs. Miller," the young policeman apologized to the laundress, who was sitting on the davenport in the living room. "I'm just as sorry as I can be. The lamp didn't hurt you, did it? And is the cat all right?"

"Everything's all right," Mrs. Miller assured him. "Take some cookies with you, young man. And please don't forget that my clothes-basket and wash have not yet been returned to me."

Peter Noble laughed and said he would remember. Then he explained that he must hurry away, but promised to call and report as soon as he had any news to tell them.

Honey Bunch went with him as far as the front door and then hurried back to the living room. From under the davenport Lady Clare peered out sulkily, but for once Honey Bunch did not pay her dearly loved pet any attention.

"Are you sick, Mrs. Miller?" cried the

little girl earnestly. "Is it your bones? Do you want me to call the doctor?"

Mrs. Miller looked at her in astonishment.

"How do you know I'm not all right, Honey Bunch?" the washerwoman asked. "I haven't said a word, have I?"

"No, but *you're sitting down!"* Honey Bunch said in great distress. "You never sit down when it's morning, Mrs. Miller. Is your leg off and on?"

Mrs. Miller tried to smile, but she could not do it very well.

"Truth to tell, Honey Bunch," she groaned, "that lamp fell on my bad leg. The one that gives me so much trouble, you know. It's beginning to swell and I don't know what to do. I can't be laid up when your mother isn't home to look after you."

"Bing-bing!" went the doorbell.

"It's Ida and Grace!" announced Honey Bunch joyfully, looking down the hall. "I'll let them in. We'll take good care of you, Mrs. Miller."

The playmates had come to suggest a meeting of the Detective Club, but when they saw Mrs. Miller sitting on the davenport they knew, just as Honey Bunch did, that something was wrong. Usually the woman was busy with either washing and ironing, or sweeping or dusting, or cooking, or cleaning silver—things like that.

"A lamp fell on her," explained Honey Bunch sadly.

Of course, Ida and Grace had to hear about everything that had happened, and Lady Clare crawled out from under the davenport and purred loudly when she was stroked and petted.

"And now I must be getting back to my work," said Mrs. Miller, who did not like to sit still very long at a time.

She rose, but sank down on the cushions again with a loud groan.

"Children, what shall I do?" she asked them, tears coming into her eyes. "I can't stand on that leg—it won't hold me up."

Poor Mrs. Miller was worried because Mr. and Mrs. Morton were away, and she said very earnestly that she could not lie flat on her back and do nothing until they reached home.

"I'll get you a drink of water," Ida offered. "A drink of water often helps."

"Put this pillow behind your back," directed Grace. "A pillow will rest you."

Honey Bunch said nothing at all, but disappeared, and in a moment Mrs. Miller heard her at the telephone in the hall.

"Honey Bunch Morton!" called the laundress, "what are you doing out there?"

"I'm getting Doctor Wood for you," Honey Bunch answered firmly. "Hello! Is this Doctor Wood's office? Will you ask him to come and see Mrs. Miller, please? Yes, at Mrs. Morton's house—he knows my daddy and mother."

"Doctor Wood's nurse says he will be here in twenty minutes," reported Honey Bunch, returning to the living room.

Mrs. Miller rubbed her leg and tried not to groan.

"Well, in a way I'm glad you've sent for him, Honey Bunch," she admitted, "though I don't know that I really need a doctor. I'm afraid he will tell me to keep off my feet and then what will happen to us? I suppose you could go and stay at Ida's house, if I couldn't do the cooking."

Honey Bunch had no intention of going to

stay with Ida, but she did not say so. She remembered that her mother had once said she was "a capital little nurse"; this was when Honey Bunch had taken care of her mother one time when she had a headache.

"If Mrs. Miller's leg is hurt, I'll take care of her," thought the little girl. "I won't go away and leave her all alone in the house, with no one to bring her cups of tea."

But Ida was delighted with the thought of having Honey Bunch come to her house.

"We can have lots of fun," she exclaimed. "We can talk over—you know what we can talk over."

Mrs. Miller, who had been dozing, gave a great jump as a piercing whistle sounded outside.

"That's only Norman Clark, Mrs. Miller," said Honey Bunch. "He's trying to learn to whistle like the postman."

"I wish that boy would move to China," the woman groaned.

Almost as soon as she had said that, she put her head back against the pillow and dozed again.

"Ida! Grace!" whispered Honey Bunch

earnestly, "come on out in the kitchen. I want to tell you something."

"Is it about a new clue?" Ida asked softly, as the two little girls followed their chum into the kitchen. Lady Clare, her tail waving, trotted happily after them.

CHAPTER VI

AN IMPORTANT CLUE

"IT'S this—" said Honey Bunch, as soon as she had closed the door between the kitchen and the dining room, so that Mrs. Miller in the room beyond could not possibly hear. "I'm the head of the house now and I have a lot to do."

"Are you the head of the house, Honey Bunch?" asked Ida respectfully.

"Why, of course she is!" Grace declared. "Her father isn't here and her mother isn't here and Mrs. Miller has a broken leg, so that makes Honey Bunch the head of the house. If anything happens to her, I'll be head of the house, won't I, Honey Bunch?"

The little Morton girl did not know about that, and Ida announced that nothing was going to happen to Honey Bunch.

"And I'm sure Mrs. Miller's leg isn't broken," added Honey Bunch anxiously, although she could not be absolutely certain since she was not a doctor.

Grace wanted to go in and "wiggle" it, for she said one could always tell if one's leg was broken by wiggling it. But Honey Bunch said no, that they must wait for the doctor.

"What we should do," she declared briskly, "is to put this house in order. It's a sight from the cat and dog chase. And I have to fix poor Mrs. Miller—her hair is half down and her apron has silver polish on it. I wish you'd clean up mother's bedroom, Ida. Fold the curtains. Don't try to hang them because someone will have to nail up the fixtures first. Then sweep up the glass in the storeroom."

Ida was always willing to help, and ready to do as she was asked. Honey Bunch knew that Grace would not take kindly to tasks that would send her away from the first floor, for Grace wanted to be there when the doctor came.

"Grace, will you fill the tea kettle and put it on to boil?" suggested Honey Bunch. "The doctor may want hot water, you know. And that's rice cooking in the double boiler. Will you see if it needs more water in the lower kettle? Mrs. Miller hates to have the double boiler burn dry."

Honey Bunch had three little aprons made just to fit her, and these she took out of a drawer in the kitchen cabinet. She gave the pink one to Ida, the yellow one to Grace, and the blue one she kept for herself. Ida took the smallest broom and the dustpan and went upstairs to make things tidy. Grace began to fill the tea kettle. Then Honey Bunch, carrying a small basin of warm water and a clean face cloth, went in to make Mrs. Miller ready for the doctor.

"You know just what to do, Honey Bunch," murmured Mrs. Miller, when her face and hands had been bathed and her soiled apron removed, and her hair made tidy as it always was, except when she was too ill to fix it. "I never saw such a handy child, never!"

Honey Bunch smiled and picked up the sofa pillows, straightened the runner on the table, and pulled the wrinkled rugs into place. Peter Noble had put the shade back on the lamp and had righted that, so when Honey Bunch had finished her tasks the living room was in order again.

"Bing-bing!" rang the doorbell.

"That's the doctor!" Honey Bunch hurried out to the kitchen to leave the basin and face cloth, and then ran to the door. Grace peeped from the kitchen, while at the head of the stairs Ida stood listening. Everyone wanted to know what Doctor Wood would say about Mrs. Miller's injured leg.

Doctor Wood was a young man, not very tall, but with broad shoulders and a smiling tanned face. He spent so much time outdoors without a hat that both summer and winter his face was sunburned. He shook hands with Honey Bunch and made her feel right away that no matter what was wrong, he could fix it.

"Well, Mrs. Miller, you don't look quite like yourself, do you?" said the man, shaking hands with her. You see, everyone who knew the washerwoman expected to see her bustling about, busy with her work.

Mrs. Miller explained what had happened, and told the doctor that the lamp had fallen on the leg which had given her trouble before. "It might at least have fallen on my good leg," she said sadly.

Doctor Wood laughed, and replied that then she might have *two* bad legs. He put down his little black bag and examined the injured leg, pressing it with his skillful fingers and trying not to hurt Mrs. Miller any more than he could possibly help. He did cause her some pain though, for once or twice she groaned.

"Is — is it broken?" asked Honey Bunch fearfully, when he had finished.

"Not broken, but badly bruised," the doctor told her, taking a roll of cotton out of his bag. "Now, I'll put something on it and bandage it up, Mrs. Miller, but you'll have to promise to stay quiet. If you get up and walk around you may bring something pretty serious upon yourself."

When the doctor had the leg neatly bound in firm white gauze, he lifted the laundress so that she lay flat on the davenport with her leg on a pillow. He put another pillow under her head and sent Honey Bunch upstairs to get a light blanket. Then he covered Mrs. Miller up warmly, gave her a pill and a glass of water, and said she should go to sleep, which she did so suddenly that Honey Bunch was surprised.

"Tired out from excitement and pain," the doctor declared. "Now, where may I wash my hands, little lady?"

He said it was not necessary to go to the bathroom, so Honey Bunch took him out to the kitchen where Ida and Grace were both tasting the rice to see if it was done. As Honey Bunch was getting a clean towel for the doctor, he suddenly said, "Has anything been worrying Mrs. Miller lately, Honey Bunch?"

"Oh my yes," Honey Bunch assured him. "The wash. And the clothes-basket. She's been dreadfully worried."

"Yes, Mrs. Morton's best dinner napkins were in the wash," Grace explained.

Doctor Wood sat down on a high stool. He looked puzzled. "One at a time," he said. "Whose wash? What clothes-basket? Why is Mrs. Miller worried?"

Honey Bunch explained about the lost basket with the clothes in it that had apparently walked right out of the Morton back yard.

"Of course it may be magic," Honey Bunch admitted doubtfully, "but I don't believe it is.

If it's magic, why can't magic bring me back my darling pink and blue checked dress?"

"I don't believe it's magic, either," said the doctor, taking out a pad and beginning to write. "Tell me about this dress, Honey Bunch. How was it made?"

Honey Bunch did not know it, but Doctor Wood disliked being asked questions when he was writing a prescription. He did not mind how much people talked, if what they said did not need an answer. So now he wrote out a prescription for Mrs. Miller while Honey Bunch was talking, and all he heard her say was at the very end, when she stated, "It had a sailor collar made of white piqué and a row of white buttons all the way down the front."

"Yes, I saw a little girl wearing a dress like that," murmured the doctor absently, tearing a sheet of paper off his pad. "Listen, Honey Bunch, somebody must take this prescription to the drug store and have it filled for Mrs. Miller. The directions will be on the bottle. Will you remember that? And tell her I'll drop in again tomorrow."

"Yes, I'll remember," promised Honey Bunch. "I know the drug store man. He has a nice cat. But where did you see a girl wearing my dress, Doctor Wood?"

"Gracious, child, I didn't say she was wearing your dress. I said I saw a girl wearing a dress like the one you described," the doctor answered. "Let me think, where did I see her? Oh, yes, over on Carter Street. I noticed the dress because it was clean and pretty and the girl's shoes were so old I thought they'd drop off her feet. She was with another child, a boy, who looked as if he'd never in his life had anything clean to wear."

Honey Bunch and Ida and Grace looked at one another.

"Well, I must be on my way," the doctor announced cheerfully. "Don't let me come tomorrow and find that prescription has been forgotten or that Mrs. Miller is walking about. If that's the case I'll roar like a raging lion and frighten every one of you out of your wits." He smiled so delightfully, that it was impossible to imagine him roaring at all.

After the doctor had gone, Honey Bunch and Ida and Grace put their heads together and held a meeting of the Detective Club. They decided that the doctor had furnished them with a very important clue which they should follow up as quickly as possible. Ida pointed out sensibly that they ought not to go in the rain. Then, too, Grace had a music lesson the next morning, so after luncheon the following day was the time decided upon. Ida and Grace went home to eat, and Honey Bunch had warm rice with cream in a blue bowl, and very good it was.

In the afternoon Norman came over. The little Morton girl had to take him up to the playroom, because Mrs. Miller said he made her nervous. Hilda was put away in a deep drawer. Honey Bunch had tucked her doll out of sight before Norman came, because she reasoned that Hunter, Peter Noble's dog, might pay another unexpected visit and romp through the house before anyone could stop him.

Norman had brought his box of magic, and went through all the tricks while Honey Bunch politely watched him. Some of them she thought he did better, some of them much worse. Anyway, she told herself, she did not think much of magic if it could not bring back the missing clothes-basket.

"Let's go over to the playground tomorrow morning," suggested Norman, when he had performed every trick. "There's a new wading pool."

"I have to be right here," Honey Bunch informed him importantly. "I have to help Mrs. Miller. Besides, Doctor Wood is coming. I have to be the head of the house."

"Well, you don't have to be head of the house in the afternoon," said Norman. "We can go over to the playground after lunch."

Honey Bunch shook her head. She could not do that.

"Ida and Grace and I are going somewhere," she said.

Norman looked excited. He tumbled his magic back into the box.

"Then I'll bet you have a new clue!" he cried. "Let me go too, Honey Bunch. I'm good at clues, you know I am. I think you girls play unfairly. I want to follow clues, too. Let me come with you, Honey Bunch."

"Four of us can't go round together," explained Honey Bunch. "If you want to follow a clue, why don't you get one of your own? You never get a clue, Norman, but you always want to follow ours. I think you ought to get some of your own."

Honey Bunch could be very firm, and though Norman teased and pleaded, she would not let him go with the detective club the next day. Finally the boy went home in a huff, banging the front door so loudly that Mrs. Miller said if her leg did not hurt her she would get up and go after him and make him shut it again more quietly.

The next morning was a busy time. Honey Bunch, under Mrs. Miller's directions, got the simple breakfast and put the rooms in order. Then Doctor Wood came and said his patient was much better. Honey Bunch had taken the prescription to the drug store, after Norman had gone home, so the doctor did not have to roar like a lion. The rain had stopped, and all the world seemed to be cheerful and bright.

"Yes, you may use the leg a little," Doctor Wood said, when Mrs. Miller asked him if she could not get up. "But you must be careful. Try to sit down for at least ten minutes every half hour. And don't be moving any mountains."

Mrs. Miller felt so much better that she made banana float for lunch, and when Honey Bunch asked if she might go out a little while, Mrs. Miller told her to run along and enjoy herself.

"Don't stay too long. I say that only because I like to know where you are," Mrs. Miller explained. "I don't want you cooped up in the house all day with me. Play outdoors all you want to, dear."

Honey Bunch found Ida and Grace waiting for her at Ida's house. The three little girls had decided to go straight to Carter Street, but that was easier said than done. None of them had liked to ask their families where Carter Street was, because mothers and fathers and brothers might say, "Why do you want to go to Carter Street?" So each member of the detective club had her own idea as to where Carter Street was, and how they could reach it.

Grace was the most confident, so the other two girls followed her for three blocks. Presently Honey Bunch noticed that they were passing familiar street signs.

"Grace, we've been past Greene Avenue

twice," Honey Bunch protested. "I'm almost sure we've seen that house before." She pointed to a little red brick dwelling across the street.

"Say, my mother said to ask you what you're selling," cried a small boy, coming up to them and staring at them as if, Ida indignantly complained, they were queer.

"We're not selling anything," Grace informed him crossly.

"Well, you keep walking up and down this street," said the boy. "My mother's been watching you. She thought you might be taking orders for pies."

After that Grace admitted she did not know how to find Carter Street and Honey Bunch decided she would try. But the streets had the most amazing habit of doubling and twisting, so that the three little girls kept coming out at the exact point at which they had started.

"How do you suppose the postman finds his way around?" asked Ida wearily.

"Have we walked a hundred miles, do you think?" Grace inquired.

Honey Bunch did not think so, though her

feet hurt her and she was tired. She saw a grocery wagon standing at the curb on which was painted in large letters, "B. Olson, Fancy Groceries, 243 Carter St."

"We can follow that wagon," suggested Honey Bunch, pointing out the letters to the other girls. "It must go to Carter Street."

They waited till the driver came out and then they trudged along, keeping their eyes on the wagon which did not go fast, because the horse hitched to it was fat and old. Honey Bunch was very tired when at last the animal turned into a brick stable and the wagon disappeared from view.

Ida pointed to a street sign on the opposite corner. "Read that!" she commanded, beginning to laugh.

"G-r-e-e-n-e A-v-e-n-u-e," Grace spelled. "Why—why, we're on Greene Avenue again. We can't seem to get off this old street."

"Then the horse didn't go to Carter Street," said Honey Bunch sadly. "I suppose his stable is on Greene Avenue." She sat down on the curb and looked up at Ida and Grace. "Do you think we're lost?" she asked wearily.

CHAPTER VII

WHERE'S CARTER STREET?

IDA said yes, of course they were lost, but Grace said no, of course they were not lost.

"How can we be lost when we know we're on Greene Avenue?" demanded Grace. "When you're lost you don't know where you are."

Honey Bunch had learned by experience that Grace and Ida could argue for hours, so she suggested that they walk a little farther.

"Let's go down that street," said Honey Bunch, pointing to the next corner. "Maybe that will take us to Carter Street."

The street did not lead to Carter Street, but it did lead to a small park. The three little girls were delighted to find an empty bench where they could sit down and rest.

"Perhaps we'll see a girl wearing your dress, Honey Bunch," said Ida, as she swung her feet comfortably.

Honey Bunch nodded. She was watching

a pigeon which was strutting back and forth on the grass.

"Is that your dress, Honey Bunch?" asked Grace in a loud whisper. She pointed to a group of children who were roller skating down a walk.

One little girl wore a pink and blue dress, but the colors were in stripes. Her dress, Honey Bunch explained, was in *checks*.

"And this dress hasn't a white collar, and mine has," she added, feeling rather glad that the skating girl did not have on the missing dress.

It would be a hard thing to have to walk up to a strange girl and tell her she was wearing your dress.

"I wish we had brought something to feed the pigeons," said Ida suddenly. "I might have asked my mother for some bread."

"We didn't know we were going to see any," Honey Bunch reminded her sensibly, "so why should we have brought bread with us?"

"There's somebody with your dress on, Honey Bunch," exclaimed Grace, pointing to a girl lying flat on the grass some distance away.

"Is it my dress?" asked Honey Bunch doubtfully.

"Of course it is," Grace said. "I can see the pink and blue checks from here. Shall I go over and ask her where she got it?"

Honey Bunch did not like this plan. Sometimes Grace forgot to be polite. Besides, Honey Bunch was not at all sure that it was her dress.

"I'll go over and walk around her, just as if I were taking a walk," Honey Bunch decided. "You stay here, girls. I'll be right back."

Ida and Grace promised to wait. Honey Bunch then walked across the grass toward the large maple tree under which the girl in the pink and blue dress was lying, reading a book. She did not glance up as the little Morton girl came near her, so Honey Bunch figured the book must be an interesting one. Mrs. Miller said that *she* was always deaf to the world when she was reading an interesting book, and Honey Bunch was sure this girl was deaf to the world.

She walked around the tree twice and came back to the bench, laughing.

"What's funny, Honey Bunch?" implored

Ida, who dearly loved a joke. "Did something funny happen?"

"Nothing happened." Honey Bunch sat down on the bench.

"Was it your dress? Did you ask the girl where she got it?" Grace demanded.

"I didn't say a word and she didn't say a word," explained Honey Bunch, still smiling. "I just looked at the girl. She must be fifteen years old and she's very fat. She couldn't wear my dress even if she had it. And the dress she has on isn't the least bit like mine anyway."

"Little girl! Oh, little girl!" called out a voice.

An automobile had suddenly stopped at the curb just behind the bench where Honey Bunch and her friends were sitting. An old lady seated in the back of the car motioned to Honey Bunch.

"Little girl, will you come here?" she called.

As Honey Bunch ran toward the machine, she saw that the old lady was holding out a large paper bag. A younger woman at the wheel, probably her daughter, smiled sweetly.

"This is bread for the pigeons," the lady explained, handing the bag to Honey Bunch. "Mary and I haven't time to feed the birds today, but they'll be so disappointed, if they don't get their bread. Will you throw this out to them, dear?"

Honey Bunch said she would, and the car drove rapidly away, as if "Mary" were in a great hurry indeed.

"Now we can feed the pigeons!" cried the little Morton girl, showing the bag to Ida. "Look at them coming—they must know that bread is put into paper bags."

The great fat pigeons were fluttering toward the bench, their lovely feathers gleaming in the sun. They were hungry, and were delighted to see the food the three girls tossed to them. Ida said that dry bread would choke her and she would not like to eat so much of it herself.

"Well, the pigeons can get a drink of water at the fountain," said Honey Bunch sensibly. "Let's go over and see it ourselves before we go home."

At some distance from their bench there was a concrete fountain, but the benches around it were filled. From where they sat the girls could see the sun shining on the water as it spurted up into the air.

"Hello, I thought you looked like Honey Bunch, but I wasn't sure," said a very cheerful voice.

Honey Bunch glanced up to see Peter Noble smiling down at her. She was a bit disappointed that the policeman did not have the clothes-basket under his arm, but of course she did not mention that. She did not wish to hurt his feelings.

"Ida! Grace! It's Peter Noble!" cried Honey Bunch.

"What are you children doing over this way?" the man asked curiously. "And how is Mrs. Miller? I meant to telephone and ask her about her injury, but I've been busy every minute today. I hope she wasn't badly hurt."

Honey Bunch explained that Mrs. Miller was better.

"You didn't scold Hunter, did you?" she asked anxiously.

"Spanked him!" said the young policeman cheerfully. "Next time he goes visiting he'll have better manners, I hope. Has the magic helped you find the clothes-basket yet?"

"No, it hasn't," Honey Bunch confessed. "But there's something we want to know very much. Where's Carter Street?"

The policeman looked puzzled, but did not ask Honey Bunch any questions.

"Carter Street is a short street," he replied. "You go down Vine, which is right over there behind you. Then you walk for one block, turn to your left, and you're on Carter Street. Hello, what's up now?"

He pointed toward the fountain, and Honey Bunch, Ida and Grace saw that people were running toward it from all over the park.

"You kids stay here." ordered Peter Noble, as he started off in a hurry.

But it was too much to ask of the three little girls that they stay away, and they began to run as fast as they could so that they reached the fountain a few seconds after Peter Noble, and in time to see him pull a very dripping small boy out of the water basin around the fountain.

"My good — goodness!" gasped Honey Bunch. "It's Norman!"

"MY GOOD-GOODNESS!" GASPED HONEY BUNCH.
"IT'S NORMAN!"

Honey Bunch: Her First Little Mystery — *Page 78*

Everyone was surprised. Peter Noble looked astonished, and Norman Clark, for all he looked half-drowned, was amazed to see who had fished him out.

"So it's you, is it?" the policeman said grimly. "What are you doing here in the fountain?"

Norman shivered, and Honey Bunch felt sorry for him.

"Oh, I have on my good suit and my mother will be mad!" wailed Norman. "I didn't mean to fall in the fountain, honest I didn't."

"All right, but what did you mean to do?" the policeman asked, keeping a tight hold on Norman as if he expected him to go in again.

"I wanted the goldfish!" Norman admitted. "The big one with the spotty tail."

"So that's it!" Peter Noble gave the culprit a little shake. "Don't you know any better than to try to take public property? Now you run home as fast as you can go and get into some dry clothes. Then tell your mother or your father just what you were trying to do, and they'll probably say a few words to you. Run!"

Norman set off at a gallop and the crowd

melted away. Peter Noble asked Honey Bunch if she remembered how to get to Carter Street, and cautioned her not to get lost. Then he went on and the three girls walked away, talking about Norman.

"He was following us, I think," said Honey Bunch. "We may not tell Norman where we're going, but he always manages to follow us. Why do you suppose he wanted a goldfish that didn't belong to him?"

"I think he wanted to see if he could catch it," Ida declared wisely. "I don't believe he meant to keep it, but he thought it would be fun to catch it by the tail. I'll bet he was very much surprised when he fell into the fountain."

"Yes, and he was surprised again when Peter Noble fished him out," laughed Grace.

Now that they had been told the way to Carter Street, they all wondered why they had not found it before. It was very near the park, a little, quiet, shabby street with only a few people walking on it. They looked carefully at every one they saw and walked the length of the street four times, but there was not a sign of a girl wearing a pink and blue checked dress.

"Well, perhaps it was a false clue," said Honey Bunch.

Just as she said that an automobile horn honked gaily and Doctor Wood drew up to the curb.

"Going my way? Want a lift?" he inquired, holding open the door of his coupe hospitably.

They were all glad to ride home. The doctor set them down at the corner of Honey Bunch's street, when they surprised him by asking how far it was from Carter Street.

"Oh, about half a mile, perhaps a little more," he answered, wondering why they should want to know that.

"Goodness, I thought we had walked twenty-five miles," Honey Bunch explained, and the doctor drove away laughing.

Ida and Grace went home without going in with Honey Bunch. Ida said that if they sat down to rest they might stay too long. Mrs. Miller, who was now sitting up on the davenport, asked Honey Bunch excitedly where she had been.

"You've been gone so long I was worried

sick," said Mrs. Miller. "Where are Ida and Grace? Did anything happen to you? Did you see Norman? His mother has been telephoning me to find out where he is."

"Oh, Norman went home a long time ago," Honey Bunch declared.

At that moment three knocks sounded on the door, which was Mrs. Clark's neighborly signal, and in rushed Norman's mother.

"Honey Bunch, have you any idea where my boy is?" she cried.

CHAPTER VIII

THE QUEER WRITING

MRS. CLARK looked so worried that Honey Bunch felt sorry for her. The little girl was also puzzled, for where could Norman be? He must have gone home, reasoned Honey Bunch, because he could not play out of doors with his clothes wringing wet.

"Honey Bunch said Norman went home a long time ago, Mrs. Clark," explained Mrs. Miller, sure that this would make the boy's mother feel comfortable.

"But he isn't home!" Mrs. Clark cried. "He hasn't come in. I haven't heard from him since lunch time. When did you see him, Honey Bunch?"

"This — this afternoon," mumbled Honey Bunch.

"Oh, after lunch? Where was he? What was he doing? Did he say he was coming home?" asked Mrs. Clark eagerly.

"He *was* going home," Honey Bunch replied truthfully. "He was running."

Then Mrs. Clark was sure that an automobile had run over Norman, and she wanted to telephone Mr. Clark and ask him what to do. This would be worse, Honey Bunch thought, than having her learn what had happened to Norman in the park, so it seemed best to tell about the goldfish.

"And Norman was soaked," said Honey Bunch, when she had finished her story, "so Peter Noble, the policeman, told him to run all the way home and put on dry clothes and then tell you. He must be home, Mrs. Clark. I'll come over with you and find him for you."

Mrs. Clark could not believe that her son was home. She was still afraid that an automobile had run over him. But Mrs. Miller was inclined to agree with Honey Bunch that Norman must be somewhere in the house.

"Bad news travels fast, Mrs. Clark," declared Mrs. Miller solemnly. "You haven't heard any bad news about Norman, so that means he is all right. He's probably afraid to tell you what happened to him."

Poor Mrs. Clark was so worried she almost

ran home and Honey Bunch trotted after her, a little worried, too.

"Norman!" called Mrs. Clark, as soon as she entered the house. "Norman, where are you? Norman, are you home, dear?"

No one answered. Mrs. Clark looked at Honey Bunch.

"I can find him," said the little girl confidently. "He's hiding. I'll have to look for him."

So first Honey Bunch went upstairs to the attic and looked around. Norman was not there. She peeped into all the rooms on the second floor, but each one was empty. Everywhere Honey Bunch went, Mrs. Clark went, too.

"Maybe he's down cellar," suggested the little girl, opening the cellar door.

She went down the steps cautiously and looked in the heater room. No sign of Norman. Then she went on to the laundry, and there he was. He was scrubbing at his suit with a large bath towel and streams of water were running out of his shoes.

"Norman Clark! I'm surprised at you!" His mother looked at him severely. "What have you to say for yourself, ruining your best suit like this?"

The boy scrubbed harder at his coat and would have rubbed a cake of laundry soap on it, only his mother rushed to him and took the soap out of his hands.

"I'm only trying to dry myself off," Norman protested.

He twisted about, and Honey Bunch saw a bit of paper fall from his pocket. She picked it up, but before she could return it to the boy, Mrs. Clark had taken him by the elbow and headed him for the stairs.

"You go straight up to your room, Norman, and undress yourself and get into bed," his mother commanded. "You stay there the rest of the day, while I try to clean your suit. When your father comes home I want you to tell him everything you've done. The idea of trying to take a goldfish out of the park fountain!"

Norman scuttled upstairs, and there was nothing for Honey Bunch to do but go home. She did not mention the paper to Mrs. Clark, because she thought that Norman's mother would not have much patience just then with any of her son's odds and ends. The little girl supposed the paper was something the boy wished to save; perhaps a part of his set of magic.

When she was out in the yard she looked at it, then tried to whistle the way Luke, the grocery boy did when he was surprised. Only Honey Bunch could not whistle. She was surprised because the paper was the one that had been wrapped around the pearl beads.

"Why, that's the reason I couldn't find it," said Honey Bunch aloud. "Norman had it! He must have picked it up and put it into his pocket. Won't Ida and Grace be s'prised!"

Honey Bunch did not mention the paper to Mrs. Miller, who was not a member of the Detective Club, but she did tell the good washerwoman that Norman would have to stay in bed for the rest of the day.

"Well, I can't say I'm sorry," the laundress replied. "Perhaps the neighborhood will have a little peace now. If I had my way, I'd put Norman to bed for five hours every day."

Honey Bunch felt that she just could not wait to show Ida and Grace the paper, but it was nearly dinner time, and of course Mrs.

Miller would need an assistant, for her leg was not well yet. The little girl set the table and afterward helped dry the dishes and then, when she had played with Lady Clare a little while, got ready for bed.

Early the next morning Honey Bunch telephoned Ida to "come over and bring Grace." She had to wait nearly an hour for them, because Ida's mother was making her two new dresses and she had to try on both of them. In the meantime, Doctor Wood came to see Mrs. Miller and wanted to know if Honey Bunch had found the clothes-basket.

"For I bank on you," said the doctor, smiling. "Anyone who can find a missing boy can certainly find a missing clothes-basket."

Then Honey Bunch knew that in some way Doctor Wood had heard about Norman. Afterward Mrs. Miller said the man had been called in by Mrs. Clark to make sure that her son had not taken cold from his plunge into the fountain.

When Ida and Grace came over the three little girls raced upstairs to the playroom, where Grace announced that the Detective Club would hold a meeting.

"To consider a clue found by our esteemed member, Honey Bunch Morton," said Grace.

"You mean Detective Morton," Ida corrected her.

Honey Bunch was so excited that she did not care by what name she was called. She carefully took the bit of paper out of a little empty box in which she had placed it, and spread it on her play table.

"I can't read it," she confessed. "Perhaps you can, Grace."

Grace and Ida both tried at the same time, and Honey Bunch was afraid the clue would be torn to bits.

"It's the paper that was wrapped around the pearl beads," Honey Bunch explained. "Do be careful, Ida. Don't jerk it, Grace. It's all blurred because Norman Clark had it in his pocket when he fell into the fountain yesterday."

"Well, I never!" Grace looked angry. "I must say that Norman Clark is too—too *fresh*. I suppose he thought that paper belonged to him."

Ida was trying to read the words in smudged ink. "I can make out something that looks like 'To my deep'," she announced, "but that doesn't make sense, does it?"

Grace took the paper and studied it, while Honey Bunch waited anxiously.

"It's 'To my dear'," declared Grace. "But the next word is all run together. It looks long, too. Maybe it is the name of a place."

Honey Bunch shook her head.

"It must be the name of a *person*," she argued. "Like this: 'to my dear Caroline'. That's a long word."

Ida took the paper again, and after puzzling a few moments said that the word was "granddaughter." That sounded right, "To my dear granddaughter."

But the rest of the words looked like a hopeless jumble and Grace suggested that they give it up. "It doesn't matter, does it?" she said. "I want to see the pearl beads again. Where's Hilda?"

Honey Bunch took her doll out of the drawer where she had hidden her away, and Grace enviously examined the pearl beads on Hilda's neck. Ida was a persevering person and refused to give up easily, so she studied the paper, turning it in all directions.

"It's not fair for your doll to have the beads all the time, Honey Bunch," Grace declared. "After all, we three found the beads. That is, we saw the trunk. I'll bet this string would look just as nice on my Rosalie as it does on your Hilda."

"Say, I think I have it!" cried Ida so suddenly that Grace almost dropped Hilda.

Honey Bunch rescued her doll and put her carefully into her rocking chair.

"This says, 'To my dear granddaughter Fanny'," read Ida, so excited that her voice trembled. " 'Each pearl is for—for——' " Ida stopped, puzzled. "The rest of it is blotted," she complained.

"Don't stop, Ida," Honey Bunch encouraged. "You can do it. Let me see—why, Ida, it says 'many happy years to come'." At this Honey Bunch gasped, because she had been able to read the blurred words almost at once.

"Here, I'll say the whole sentence for you!" cried Grace, who hated to be left out of anything. She took the paper from Ida and read in a loud voice: "To my dear granddaughter Fanny. Each pearl is for many happy years to come."

The children looked at one another. What did the words mean? Who had written them? Honey Bunch was the first to make up her mind.

"I think it was Fanny's birthday," she decided. "And her grandma gave her the pearl beads. Just the way Ida's grandma gave her blue beads on her last birthday."

Ida looked at the necklace on the doll.

"Mine aren't half as pretty as those," she said wistfully.

"We're going to let our dolls take turns wearing them," Honey Bunch assured her generously. "Grace wants Rosalie, her big doll, to wear them and you, Ida, can have them for your best doll Frances. I think you ought to have them first, because Fanny is another name for Frances. Mrs. Miller told me. Your doll can wear Fanny's beads first, Ida."

"Good afternoon! Ladies and Gentlemen, allow me to introduce to you Professor Ritz-Carlton!" cried Norman Clark, just then walking into the room without bothering to knock at the door. He had come up the stairs so quietly that no one had heard him.

Honey Bunch hastily rolled up the bit of paper and put it back in the box. She did not want Norman to get hold of it again, because for all she knew, he might fall into another fountain.

"I've come to amuse you," said the professor kindly. "If you'll keep perfectly quiet I'll perform my best magic tricks for you. Ladies and Gentlemen, we shall now observe the coin trick."

Norman had three metal coins, which were real money. These he declared he could make disappear while the audience watched. He showed them the coins on the palm of his hand and begged them to watch him carefully.

"Um-gla!" he cried loudly. "Perla-perla-punka-pump!"

Norman shot his hand into the air and the coins fell with a clump on the bare floor. He dived for them, then stood back, waiting for his audience, who had also dived after the coins, to come upright again.

"The pearl beads!" cried Ida. "Oh-oh, the beads are gone! Honey Bunch, we've lost the lovely beads!"

CHAPTER IX

ANOTHER FIND

HONEY BUNCH stared at the play table. Nothing was on it except the box that held Norman's magic tricks. Ida had seen Honey Bunch put the string of beads on the table ready for her to take home.

"Was it the magic?" asked Ida fearfully. "Did magic make the beads disappear?"

"Probably they dissolved," Grace said wisely. "Vanished into the air, you know." And she stared around the playroom as if she expected to see some of the pearl beads floating in the air.

But Honey Bunch believed in magic only up to a certain point. She did not believe, for instance, that Norman could make a string of pearl beads vanish into the air. She suspected that he had something to do with their disappearance, but she doubted if he had used magic.

"Norman Clark," she said severely, "roll

down your sleeve. Yes, your blouse sleeve. You roll it down *now.*"

The boy pretended not to hear.

"Maybe I can find the beads for you, if I use my magic," he declared. "Want me to try? Ladies and Gentlemen——"

"Don't be silly," scolded Honey Bunch. "You roll down your blouse sleeve. You didn't have it rolled up when you started to do the coin trick."

Norman saw that Honey Bunch was in earnest, so very slowly he began to unroll the sleeve of his red and white striped blouse. Out dropped the string of beads. The sun glinted on the stones in the clasp as the necklace lay on the floor, and they winked like bits of fire.

"Well, what do you know about that?" Norman pretended to be very much surprised.

Honey Bunch hastily picked up the beads and handed them to Ida.

"You keep them one day for your doll," she directed, "and then give them to Grace. Grace will give them back to me. That way we'll all take turns."

"Where does my turn come in?" demanded Norman. "Don't I get anything?"

"You wouldn't want to wear beads, would you?" Honey Bunch argued patiently. "And you haven't any doll to wear beads, so what would you do with them?"

Norman did not know, but his feelings were hurt. He felt "left out," he said. After Ida and Grace had gone, Honey Bunch tried to cheer up the small boy. Perhaps, she admitted to herself, he had a right to feel hurt, because he was not the head detector in the Detective Club, and also because his magic did not seem to be going well.

"Do you want to go to Jake Silberman's with me next time, Norman?" asked Honey Bunch, who had a plan of her own. "I mean, just you and I? We could hunt in that trunk again and perhaps find a clue to the clothes-basket."

"When is 'next time'?" asked the lad.

Honey Bunch had to think about that. She said it was too late to go that day, because it was lunch time now and in the afternoon she had promised to do three errands for Mrs. Miller. The doctor would not let the laundress walk to the store or even much around the house. He said she must be careful. So

Honey Bunch had to go to the grocer's and the butcher's and the hardware man's for her.

"But tomorrow morning we might go to Jake Silberman's," said Honey Bunch. "You come over right after breakfast, Norman. Perhaps we'll find some clues."

"I could come before breakfast," suggested Norman hopefully.

"No one goes anywhere before breakfast," explained Honey Bunch, "and we can't have company for breakfast when Mrs. Miller's leg hurts her. No, you come over afterward, and we'll start right away."

The next morning, when Honey Bunch came downstairs, Mrs. Miller asked, "Why is Norman Clark sitting on our front step?"

The little girl peeped through one of the front windows. Sure enough, there on the front steps sat the boy.

"He's waiting for me," Honey Bunch said. "I told him not to come here until after breakfast."

Mrs. Miller laughed and said that Norman must think they had breakfast at five o'clock in the morning. But when Honey Bunch had finished her cereal and toast and was ready to go, Mrs. Miller gave her a jelly doughnut to hand to Norman.

The two children ran most of the way to the Silberman yard. They both felt that they wanted to spend the whole morning there, and that it would be a pity to waste any time getting to the place. They looked around to see if the bearded Jake was anywhere in sight before they scuttled through the gap in the fence and made a bee-line for the trunk, which was just where they had left it.

"Why do you want to fuss with that trunk?" asked Norman. "I thought you were looking for the clothes-basket and the wash. You don't expect to find your pink and blue dress in the trunk, do you?"

"No," said Honey Bunch, "I don't. But I want to see *what* is in the trunk. Maybe we can find some more beads."

Though they looked carefully, and Norman almost stood on his head to search the inside, they found no more beads. Honey Bunch insisted upon running her hands over the paper lining, after Norman had finished feeling around in the trunk. To her astonishment the paper cracked and a little drawer slipped out. Honey Bunch peered in.

"There's a fan!" she cried. She pulled out a small object and Norman saw that it was indeed a fan.

"Pooh! What's a fan?" he said crossly. "That isn't any good. It's only paper, anyway."

Honey Bunch looked at the little object which was made of soft, faded pink paper. The sticks of the fan were black. There were pictures printed on them, but they were faded like the paper itself.

"I like it!" announced Honey Bunch firmly. "I'm going to keep it. I'll put it away in my treasure box."

"Not so fast, not so fast, young lady!" a gruff voice sounded behind the children. "What are you doing in my yard? Who told you you could come here and help yourself to my property?"

Honey Bunch and Norman stared, both of them really frightened. They had not heard Jake Silberman until he spoke to them, and he looked anything but pleased to find two little strangers going through a trunk that belonged to him. His black eyes snapped angrily and his gray beard bobbed up and down as his chin moved.

"Please," said Honey Bunch bravely, "we're only looking in the trunk. I found this fan—it's pretty."

"Have you been here before?" Mr. Silberman questioned gruffly.

"Yes, sir, once," she answered, for Norman seemed to have lost his power to speak. "We found some beads. We didn't think you wanted them, because you'd thrown away the trunk, hadn't you?"

As Honey Bunch talked, Jake Silberman kept looking at her and at Norman. When he spoke again, his voice did not sound so cross.

"Why, you're just a couple of kids," he said. "I thought you were older. I have a lot of trouble with older boys and girls who try to run off with my tires and sell them for what they can get. Any selling that's done, I intend to do it, see? But I don't mind if you keep any little things you've found—that fan, for instance. And if the beads are pretty enough to keep, they're yours. Maybe if you look around the junk piles you'll find some more small stuff you'd like."

Norman, deciding that the second-hand

dealer was not going to "make a fuss," plucked up his courage and said respectfully, "I don't suppose you have a knife you don't want? An old knife?"

"A knife?" Jake Silberman repeated. "Why, no, I don't know that I have a knife. Do you plan to scalp some Indians, young fellow?"

Norman explained that what he wanted was a pen-knife to carry in his pocket.

"I thought you might have one you didn't want and I could have it to remember you by," he added.

"Well, you come up to the house with me," the second-hand dealer said kindly, "and I'll look around. I don't keep knives out here in the yard because they might get rusty."

Honey Bunch and Norman followed him to the house. To get there they had to walk around heaps of old automobile tires, piles of rusty iron, and heaps of broken furniture, old boxes and more trunks.

Mrs. Silberman was watering some plants in a window box when they reached the place. She looked a little surprised to see the two children, but she nodded and smiled to them, when her husband explained that he had promised the little boy a pen-knife. Mrs. Silberman was a tall, thin woman, who wore a green dress and had her hair bundled into a blue sweeping cap.

"I think you'll find some knives in the drawer of that old desk, Jake," she suggested. "Only you must remember that the child may cut himself."

Her husband looked at her and smiled.

"Well, there's that pearl-handled one without any blades," he said. "Wouldn't that do?"

Norman was alarmed. He did not want anything without blades, and he said so.

"I plan to carve things with it," he explained. "Maybe I can whittle a clipper ship if it's a good knife."

Jake Silberman grunted. He opened a drawer in a desk and from it took a little knife with a pearl handle and two blades.

"Now, if you cut yourself, don't let your mother blame me," he said solemnly.

Before Norman could express his delight, Honey Bunch, who stood facing the door, cried, "Oh, Peter Noble! How nice to see you! Look, Norman!"

The young patrolman was so tall and straight that his head almost touched the top of the doorway. He said "Hello" to the children, but Honey Bunch noticed he did not ask how Mrs. Miller was or say that his dog sent his love to Lady Clare. Peter Noble usually made some joke like that, but today he did not seem to have much to say.

"When you have time, Jake," he nodded to the second-hand man, "I'd like to ask you a question or two."

Mrs. Silberman brought forward a chair.

"Sit down, sir," she said politely. "Jake isn't going anywhere this morning. I'm sure he'll talk to you now."

Honey Bunch saw that Peter Noble shook his head. He did not wish to sit down. The little girl missed his cheerful smile.

"Come on, Norman," she whispered, pulling the boy by the sleeve. "We have to go home now. Good-bye, Mr. Silberman, and thank you for everything."

As soon as they were out of the yard, Honey Bunch turned earnestly to her playmate.

"Do you think Mr. Silberman is going to get arrested, Norman?" she asked.

CHAPTER X

NEW FRIENDS

NORMAN decided it was about time he acted like a detective, at least the way he thought a detective ought to act.

"Yes, he'll probably be arrested," said the little fellow gloomily. "And he'll go to jail for five years, perhaps six. Six years from today maybe we'll see Jake Silberman coming out of jail."

Honey Bunch was horrified. Six years must be a very long time to be in jail, she thought.

"Oh, oh, will Peter Noble take him right away and never let him out?" she asked, looking ready to cry. "Why, that nice policeman ought not to do a thing like that."

Norman said that Peter probably did that often. Honey Bunch felt very sorry for Jake Silberman, until lunch time, when she happened to mention to Mrs. Miller what the boy had said.

"That's only some more of Norman's nonsense," Mrs. Miller declared. "Policemen haven't anything to do with the length of time people stay in prison. I wish you wouldn't waste your time listening to that lad, Honey Bunch. He's at the bottom of all my worry."

Honey Bunch did not want Mrs. Miller to worry.

"Is it about the wash?" asked the little girl sympathetically. "Is Norman at the bottom of the wash, Mrs. Miller?"

"Well, he's the real reason why we lost it and the clothes-basket," the laundress said. "If I hadn't come into the house to see what that boy was up to, no one would have had a chance to steal even a handkerchief."

"Doctor Wood said you mustn't fret," Honey Bunch reminded her.

"That's easy for him to say," returned Mrs. Miller. "It isn't his wash that's disappeared. I'll feel fine, won't I, when your mother comes home? I'll have to tell her the family's best clothes have been stolen."

Honey Bunch was sure her mother would know it was not the laundress's fault. While she was trying to comfort the washerwoman the telephone rang. It was Ida Camp.

"I'll bring back the beads this afternoon, Honey Bunch," said Ida. "Grace wants them, you know. But I don't want her to take them until you see me give them to her. Detectives always have a witness, you know."

Honey Bunch thought Ida was very clever, and as soon as her fellow members arrived Honey Bunch took them up to the playroom, where they could hold a meeting.

"Fellow Detectives, I have some things to tell you," confided Honey Bunch. "Maybe they're not clues, but they're interesting. Norman and I went down to Jake Silberman's this morning."

Of course Ida and Grace were interested, but Grace could not forget the pearl beads.

"Give them to me, Honey Bunch," she urged. "It's my turn to have them. I want to go home and put them on Rosalie. Then I'll come right back."

Honey Bunch gave her friend the necklace and begged her not to lose it. Sometimes Grace was careless, but she promised to be "extra careful" this time. She dashed home, and Honey Bunch told Ida about the trip she and Norman had made to the second-hand dealer's place.

"Here's the fan," said Honey Bunch, taking it carefully out of her treasure box. "Norman has a knife, but he really asked for it. I think Mr. Silberman is nice, and I hope Peter Noble didn't arrest him."

Ida said she hoped so, too. Then in came Grace, completely out of breath from running. She had to hear everything all over again, and though she said she did not think much of the fan, Honey Bunch noticed that she asked if there were any more in the trunk.

"I guess there's not a thing left in the trunk," Honey Bunch declared earnestly. "Norman and I would have found them if there were any more there. Don't you think we ought to go to Carter Street again, girls? Now we know the way we can get there easily, and we might see my dress on a girl."

"Yes," agreed Ida. "We don't have to tell Norman, do we?"

"He isn't home—that's the reason he isn't over here," Honey Bunch explained seriously.

"His suit shrank up and his mother took him downtown to buy him another one."

The three little girls told Mrs. Miller they would not be gone very long, and then set off for Carter Street. This time they had no trouble finding it, but, as Honey Bunch observed, the people who lived in Carter Street did not seem to care a great deal about fresh air.

"They never seem to be around, do they?" Ida puzzled. "Well, I think we ought to walk up and down a little while, as if we were just enjoying the view."

The little girls did this for several minutes, until Grace said her shoe rubbed her heel, and Ida said she was tired, so Honey Bunch decided that if any little child were wearing her dress she must have gone downtown, and perhaps would not be back until supper time.

"Let's sit on the steps of that church," suggested Honey Bunch, pointing toward a gray stone building on one corner. "We can walk some more after we get rested."

They crossed the street and seated themselves on the smooth, curving steps of the church. The building was covered with ivy.

"There are pigeons here, too," said Ida, pointing to some birds that were strutting on the pavement. "I wish we had something to feed them."

"They probably live in the church tower," Grace remarked, yawning. "Goodness, how my heel hurts! I'll bet it has a blister on it. What are you staring at, Honey Bunch?"

"Peter Noble," said Honey Bunch placidly. "He's in that car."

"That isn't Peter Noble," Grace contradicted. "This man has on a gray suit. And there are some people with him. The other man isn't a policeman, either. See, they're getting out."

"It *is* Peter Noble," said Ida, as a girl and two men stepped out of a car in front of the church.

The three came directly toward the children, and even though Grace could not believe in a Peter Noble without his uniform, she had to when he stopped and said, "Do my eyes deceive me? What have we here?"

"Pigeons," said the other young man, smiling. "Three little pigeons. Or perhaps they're canaries—what do you think, Ruth?"

The young lady smiled at Honey Bunch, and it was a lovely smile. She was a very pretty person, dressed all in gray from her suede shoes to her silk hat.

"Why, I think they're three tired little girls who sat down to rest," she said, and her voice reminded Honey Bunch of the brook on the farm where Stub, her cousin, lived. The water rushed with that same soft, swift sound.

Peter Noble led the others around the three children, and as he passed Honey Bunch he patted her on the head.

"This is my sister," he said proudly. "We're taking her to call on the rector."

Ruth Noble turned and smiled again at the group.

"Why, you're the children Peter has been telling us about!" she exclaimed. "Fred, you recall my brother telling us all about the missing clothes-basket."

Peter Noble waved his hand.

"Miss Honey Bunch Morton, Miss Ida Camp, and Miss Grace Winters," he recited. "Mr. Frederic T. Paull. Mr. Paull is the fiance of my sister Ruth," he added.

Honey Bunch stood up, her eyes shining.

"If he's a fiance, you're going to be married to him," she cried joyfully. "Oh, mayn't we come in and see it, *please?*"

Ruth Noble laughed and said that she was not to be married *now.*

"We're here to make arrangements for the wedding," she said. "It will be very quiet—nothing for you to see, dear. If you care to come in with us it will be all right. But you must promise to be quiet."

"I'll attend to them," said Peter Noble.

Though Honey Bunch knew he was just pretending to be severe, his voice made her shiver a little. He could make it sound so harsh and stern.

"Maybe that's the way he talks to Jake Silberman," thought the little girl.

She wished she could ask Peter what he had done with Jake Silberman, but this did not seem to be the place to ask questions like that. Timid Ida was clinging close to Honey Bunch's hand, and even Grace was quiet as they entered the dim, still church.

Peter Noble and Fred Paull walked one on either side of Ruth as they went down the wide centre aisle. After them trotted the three little girls, feeling as if they were going to what Honey Bunch called a "truly" wedding. When they reached the front of the church they went around the altar and into a little room where a gray-haired man was seated at a desk.

"Well, my dear, you're on time," he said to Ruth as he rose to greet her, and shake hands with Peter and Fred.

"Three friends of ours who want to listen, Doctor Marshall," said Peter, drawing Honey Bunch, Ida and Grace forward. "They're going to sit on this small sofa and the first one that speaks, out she goes."

There was a little red velvet sofa at one side of the room, and the children perched themselves up on that. Then, for perhaps twenty minutes, they listened quietly but intently as Ruth and her fiance and Peter talked. They arranged the day for the wedding and the hour. They decided on how many were to be present. They talked about the music and about who was to teach Ruth's Sunday School class while she was on her wedding trip. Then Doctor Marshall announced that he had an appointment and must leave them.

"You'd better let your best man show you our church, Mr. Paull," the rector suggested. "You'll be less nervous if you feel at home Saturday."

After the rector had gone, everyone went into the church and Mr. Paull asked Ruth what kind of flowers she would like to wear.

"What do you think, Honey Bunch?" asked the pretty bride to be. "Shall I have larkspur, or——or——"

"Well, four o'clocks would be nice, but you can't have those at eleven o'clock in the morning, I s'pose," said Honey Bunch regretfully. "We have them in our garden. Morning glories would be 'propriate, wouldn't they?"

Ruth said yes, and laughed. She explained that morning glories closed up almost as soon as they were picked, though.

"I think I'll have larkspur," she decided. "I'm to be married in blue and they'll go well with my suit."

"Oh, aren't you going to wear a veil and a train and carry a bouquet with ribbons on it?" demanded Grace, quite horrified. "My aunt did and she had orange blossoms."

"This is going to be a quiet wedding," explained Fred Paull. "No fuss, no feathers. Just a few relatives and friends. Ruth and I like things done quietly."

"I'm going to have that same kind of a wedding when I grow up," Ida confided, suddenly finding her tongue. "And when the minister marries us, all he'll have to say will be 'Do you?' and I'll say 'Why certainly', and we won't need any feathers at all."

Peter Noble began to laugh, but his sister told him to be quiet.

"I wonder if you children would like to see my wedding without any 'feathers'?" she asked seriously. "There's no reason why they shouldn't come, is there, Fred?"

"Not if they can stand it without the feathers," Fred Paull chuckled.

So then and there Ruth Noble invited Honey Bunch and Ida and Grace to attend her wedding on Saturday morning at eleven o'clock. How thrilled they were, to have a wedding to look forward to!

As soon as the three little girls found themselves out in the street again, Honey Bunch said in a whisper, "Do you know what I think? We ought to give Ruth a wedding present."

"We haven't any money," objected Grace.

"We could give her the beads," whispered Honey Bunch. "The pearl beads we found in the trunk."

Both Ida and Grace were delighted with this idea and Grace was willing to take the necklace off her doll at once and put it in a box. The children could hardly wait to reach Grace's house, they were so pleased with their plan, so they ran almost the whole way, even though the sun was hot.

"Look!" cried Honey Bunch, stopping short as they turned a corner. "Look down that way! See that girl? She's wearing my pink and blue dress—the one that was in the wash when someone stole it!"

CHAPTER XI

ONE MYSTERY SOLVED

AT FIRST Ida and Grace looked in the wrong direction and could not see any girl.

"Where, Honey Bunch?" implored Ida. "Oh, where's the girl? I don't see her. Where is she?"

"There!" Honey Bunch pointed again. "No, not that way. *This* way. See, a boy's with her."

"I see her!" Grace cried. "Come on, she's a clue. What are you waiting for? Hurry. We must follow the clue."

Detective Morton started to run, and after her raced Detectives Camp and Winters. As they came nearer the little girl they could see that she was crying. An older boy, perhaps her brother, was pulling her along and scolding her about something.

"Wait a minute!" Honey Bunch had to stop for breath, and she wanted to say something too. "I don't know what to tell her about my dress. Maybe she doesn't know it's mine."

"How can you be so silly!" Grace was out of patience. "Of course she knows it's your dress. She took it, didn't she? All you have to say is 'Give me my dress. The idea of your stealing it!' "

That sounded all right, but Honey Bunch did not think she could do it. Anyway, what happened next so surprised her that she did not say a word to the little girl.

The three "detectives" were walking a few feet behind the crying girl and the little boy who was pulling her along. As they watched, the two children turned into a narrow alley.

"I'll bet they live there," whispered Ida.

Honey Bunch ran ahead and reached the alley just in time to see the girl and the boy climbing up a rickety stairway. The steps were evidently at the back of a dilapidated old house which looked as if it might tumble down any minute.

"Is that where they live?" whispered Ida, who had followed Honey Bunch.

"Yes, I think so," her playmate nodded.

Grace, who had stopped to tie her shoes,

came rushing up. When the others showed her the stairway she wanted to go up and see the home of the children they had followed. Honey Bunch said she did not think this was a good plan, however.

"All right, then, what shall we do?" asked Grace crossly. "I've never heard of being a detective, and then not following a clue."

"What I think we should do," said Honey Bunch, who refused to quarrel, "is to go and tell Peter Noble. Maybe he will come back with us."

This was such a good idea that even Grace was pleased. The three chums took hold of one another's hands and scurried back the same way they had come. When they reached the church, breathless, they were delighted to find the Noble car still at the curb. Ruth was standing on the steps with her fiance, but her brother was not in sight.

"Why, here are our little wedding guests back again!" cried Fred Paull, his eyes twinkling. "Do you think it's Saturday now?"

"We must see Peter Noble," Honey Bunch announced with dignity. "We have something to tell him."

Just then the policeman came out of the church and closed the heavy door behind him. He looked surprised to see the three girls, but he listened politely, even when they all talked at once.

"Are you sure this child had on your dress, Honey Bunch?" the young man asked. "Could you identify it? I mean, could you say positively that it is yours?"

"My, yes," declared Honey Bunch. "I *know* it's my dress. We didn't go in and ask her for it, though, because we thought the boy might hurt us."

"I'll go back with you," said Peter gravely. "You did right to come after me. Never go into a strange house unless you are sure you'll find friends there. Fred, please take Ruth home. I won't need the car."

Miss Noble offered to drive her brother and the children to the alley house, but Peter said it would be better for him to walk. Then he set off, taking such long steps that the three little detectives had to run to keep up with him.

"Now, I don't want any of you to say a word until I ask you to talk," he said, stopping short at the foot of the wabbly stairway. "Let me handle this. Keep away from that railing, for it looks as if it might give way any minute."

Indeed, Peter seemed to worry more about the stairs than he did about what he would find at the top of them. Honey Bunch did not wonder at that, for the steps were so old that some of the boards had rotted and one had dropped out entirely. It would be easy to fall through that on a dark night, Honey Bunch thought.

At the top of the stairs was a wooden door, painted green. Peter Noble knocked, but no one answered. Then he turned the handle and opened the door. He stepped into a room and the three little girls silently followed him.

Facing them, backed against the wall, were the girl and boy they had seen on the street. The girl was not crying, but she looked as if she might any moment. The boy held a towel in his hand. Honey Bunch recognized the initial "M" worked in one corner. She saw that it was a bath towel, one missing from her home.

"Why didn't you answer when I knocked?"

asked Peter Noble, looking straight at the boy.

"I thought you were the rent man," the lad replied. "We haven't any rent money. I can't help it."

Then Peter began to ask more questions, while Honey Bunch tried to listen and at the same time see what was in the room. There was not much to see—just a table and two chairs, a bed in one corner, an old cook stove and a clothes-line on which dangled some garments. There was only one window, and that had no curtain.

"Do they have only one room to live in?" whispered Ida.

Honey Bunch nodded "Yes," and frowned at Ida for her to keep quiet.

"So your name's Willie Nock, is it?" asked Peter Noble. "How old are you? Fourteen? You look small for that. Is this your sister? Her name's Tootsy? Are you mean to her? Is that what makes her cry?"

Tootsy was weeping again, and it made everyone uncomfortable to hear her.

"She has an ear-ache," said Willie. "And she's kind of hungry, too, I guess."

"Perhaps it's a guilty conscience," the policeman returned sternly. "Honey Bunch, do you see anything that belongs to the wash Mrs. Miller says was stolen from your yard?"

Before the little Morton girl could answer, Willie Nock gasped. "Oh, are you a policeman?" he asked. "We didn't mean to steal the things, honest we didn't."

"Are those your clothes, Honey Bunch?" asked Peter, pointing to the clothes-line and apparently not paying any attention to what the boy said.

"Yes," Honey Bunch said firmly, "that's my green bloomer dress. And that little girl has on my blue and pink dress. But I don't see my daddy's silk pajamas."

"Oh, Willie put those away in a newspaper," cried Tootsy eagerly. "Mr. Denty wanted to wear them, but Willie wouldn't let him. And we never touched the sheets and pillow cases and table things. We used two of the towels, but that's all. We took care of the things, didn't we, Willie?"

Peter Noble sat down on one of the chairs and looked at the Nock boy.

"Suppose you tell me how you came to take a wash that didn't belong to you," he suggested. "Where are your parents? I should think they'd tell you that taking things that don't belong to you is called stealing. People get into trouble for that."

Willie Nock twisted the towel in his hands. He was very thin, but Honey Bunch did not think he seemed like a bad boy.

"It's like this," he replied. "My mother takes in washing and I get the clothes for her. I was out one day on my way to get Mrs. Tucker's work and bring it to Mother. It was a new place. The lady had moved, and I'd never been there before. I got lost, but when I saw a basket of clothes in the yard I thought it was her home so I took them."

"These clothes were washed and ready to be ironed," Peter declared. "Didn't you expect to get dirty clothes for your mother to wash?"

"She just irons for Mrs. Tucker," explained the boy. "You see, we haven't a good place to hang out clothes and some ladies won't let my mother do their washing, but they like to have her iron. Mrs. Tucker used to leave her clothes-basket out for me, if she wanted to go downtown before I got there."

"Well, didn't your mother know you'd got the wrong wash when you brought it home?" suggested the policeman.

Tears came into Willie Nock's eyes, and Honey Bunch thought *he* was going to cry. Although he did not, his voice sounded a little odd.

"When I got back, the ambulance was down in the alley and men were carrying my mother out to it," he said. "Her dress had caught fire from the stove. They thought she would die from the burns, but she's getting better; only she can't come home for a long time. I have to take care of Tootsy now."

Honey Bunch and Ida and Grace felt very sorry for the boy and they could see that Peter felt sorry, too. But he told Willie to finish his story.

"Two days after my mother was taken to the hospital, Mrs. Tucker came to see why I hadn't come to get her wash," said Willie. "I told her I had, but she said that basket wasn't hers. Then I started out to take back the clothes I had brought home and I couldn't find the house. I looked for three days. I couldn't remember what street it was on, or how the house looked, or anything.

"The lady down stairs, Mrs. Denty, sometimes gives us things to eat. I told her about the clothes and she said that if I couldn't find the owner I might as well keep the things and use them. She wanted the silk pajamas for her husband, but I said no, I'd have to ask my mother first. But my mother can't see any one yet and Tootsy had nothing to wear, so I thought it wouldn't hurt if I put one of the dresses on her. I used two of the towels to wash her face with. Mrs. Denty borrowed the towel we had and I couldn't let Tootsy go looking so dirty."

For a moment Peter Noble did not say anything. Willie stared at him anxiously and the three little visitors stared, too. They were wondering if the policeman would scold this boy and his little sister.

"Where you made your big mistake," he said at last, "was in taking Mrs. Denty's advice. Just because you can't find an owner doesn't mean that whatever you find belongs to you. Never give up trying to locate the person to whom property of any kind rightfully belongs. Will you remember that? I don't believe your mother, had she been home, would have allowed your sister to wear these dresses, do you?"

"No sir, I don't believe she would," Willie admitted. "I'm awfully sorry. I'll wash them and take them back. I don't know how to iron, or I'd do that."

"Never mind washing and ironing. Just put everything into the basket and leave it alone till I tell you what to do with it," the policeman instructed him kindly. "And now what next? Have you had your meals regularly since your mother has been in the hospital?"

Willie shook his head. He pointed to a can on the shelf over the stove.

"I gave Tootsy all the condensed milk we had yesterday," he confided. "That can's empty, but I thought if I washed it out with water there might be some milk in it—enough for her supper. We haven't any money, because mother can't do any washing, you see."

Peter Noble put his hand into his pocket and pulled out a handful of change. He selected four quarters and held them out to Honey Bunch.

"Honey Bunch, there's a grocery store a block from here. I saw it as we passed," he said. "Will you and Ida and Grace go there and get two quarts of milk and two loaves of bread? You'll have to promise not to drop the milk bottles, not to fall down those terrible stairs, and not to lose the money. Now, do you think you can fill that large order?"

"Oh, yes!" Honey Bunch laughed delightedly. "Come on, girls, let's hurry. Tootsy won't cry when she has some good bread and milk to eat. Put the money in my pocket, Peter. No one loses money out of a coat pocket."

So away dashed Honey Bunch and her faithful friends, eager to get bread and milk for the hungry children.

CHAPTER XII

HONEY BUNCH'S STORY

HONEY BUNCH remembered the grocery store they had passed, and as she and Ida and Grace carefully picked their way down the old stairs, the little Morton girl tried to describe the place.

"Oh, Honey Bunch!" called Peter Noble, just as the three children safely reached the ground. "Get some oranges, too, will you?"

"All right!" Honey Bunch waved her hand to show she understood, then broke into a run, because it seemed so important to her to get the food right away.

The grocery store was a small one and dreadfully crowded. It was not very well lighted, either, and there were so many things hanging from the ceiling that Ida was sure something would drop on their heads. At first the girls thought there was no one in the place, but when Grace coughed a little, a stooped old man bobbed up from behind the counter, very much like a jack-in-the-box.

"Yes, lady, what can I do for you, lady?" he asked politely.

"We want two quarts of milk and two loaves of bread," Honey Bunch answered. "And please tell us how much your oranges are."

The old man hobbled to the back of the store and returned with two bottles. He opened a wire cage and took out two loaves of bread, wrapped in waxed paper.

"Oranges are twenty-three cents, twenty-seven cents and forty cents a dozen," he said rapidly.

"Well, you see," Honey Bunch explained, "we have to know how much the bread and milk are, so we can tell if we have enough money for oranges."

The grocer began to figure on a paper bag.

"Well, lady," he said, "the milk and bread come to 44 cents. You get three cents back on each bottle, if you return 'em. Want some oranges?"

Grace and Ida looked at Honey Bunch.

"How much is 44 cents from one dollar?" Honey Bunch asked cautiously.

"Fifty-six," the grocer told her. "You can get one dozen of the best forty cent oranges if you want 'em."

Grace had been counting on her fingers and now she said quickly, "Honey Bunch, you get two dozen of the twenty-seven cent oranges. They have more juice in them, my mother says. I'll carry them for you."

Honey Bunch was grateful for any advice, and said she would have two dozen of the cheaper oranges. When they were counted out into a bag Grace took it and Ida picked up the bread, leaving the bottles of milk for Honey Bunch to carry.

"Ninety-eight cents, please, lady," said the grocer.

Honey Bunch put her hand into her coat pocket. A startled look came over her face. The money was not there! She felt in the other pocket. No money!

"Have you lost it?" stammered Grace in alarm.

"I *couldn't* lose it," Honey Bunch argued. "Peter put it in my pocket. It couldn't fall out."

The grocer said that perhaps the money

had dropped when she was running. "Was it a dollar bill?" he asked.

"No, four quarters," Honey Bunch told him. "They didn't fall out, for we would have heard them when they hit the pavement."

"Let me feel in your pocket," said Ida.

"It would be too bad if we couldn't take the food to those children, wouldn't it?" Grace murmured. She was inclined to look on the dark side of things, so her mother said.

Ida felt in Honey Bunch's coat pocket on the right hand side, but no money was there. Then she tried the left hand one.

"Why, Honey Bunch, there's a hole in the lining!" cried Ida. "I do believe those quarters went through the hole!"

Ida and Grace and the grocer all felt of the hem at the bottom of Honey Bunch's coat. Sure enough, the four quarters had slipped through the hole in the pocket and were now down there.

"I'll have to cut a stitch or two to get them out," said the grocer, "but I'll put a safety pin in it for you. That will hold till you get home."

He cut a few stitches in the hem and the four quarters dropped to the floor with a little clinking noise. The man put a safety pin in the lining and gave Honey Bunch the two cents in change which she put into the pocket on the other side where there was no hole.

"Come again, ladies," said the grocer, holding open the door for his three customers who filed out, each holding a bag in her arms.

They could not hurry for fear they would drop the milk or spill the oranges. As they were walking very carefully back to the alley, Honey Bunch saw a familiar auto.

"There's Doctor Wood!" she cried, and at the same moment the doctor recognized her.

"Well, you look as if you might need a lift!" he called, stopping his car. As the little girls came up to him, he added, "Since when has Mrs. Miller taken to having her marketing done over in this section? And don't the grocers deliver any more?"

"We found the wash!" Honey Bunch held tightly to the milk bottles, but her voice sounded excited. "We found the wash, Doctor Wood. And the clothes-basket. Willie Nock took it, and then he couldn't find our house to put it back. His mother is burned in the hospital and his little sister has the earache. She cries all the time."

"Yes, and they're hungry. Peter sent us out to buy bread and milk for them," said Ida.

"And oranges," Grace added.

Doctor Wood looked puzzled, but he asked a few questions and soon had the whole story of the "lost and found wash," as he called it, straight in his mind.

"Hop in, children, and I'll drive you the rest of the way," he promised. "I think I'll take a look at this Tootsy, too. Where did she get a name like that? If she has an earache, perhaps I can fix it for her, and give her something to ease the pain."

Honey Bunch, scrambling into the car, beamed upon him.

"I think doctors are so nice!" she told him. "Doctors and policemen, too. If I can't be a policewoman when I grow up I mean to be a doctor. Girls can be doctors, can't they, Doctor Wood?"

The man said they certainly could, and he told about three women doctors he knew. Before he had finished they had reached the alley house and the rest of the story would have to wait till next time, he said. He carried the milk up the stairs and Honey Bunch helped Grace carry the oranges.

Peter Noble heard their footsteps and opened the door. He was surprised to see the doctor, whom he knew, but was very much pleased to hear that the kind man wanted to see if he could make Tootsy Nock more comfortable. While he was examining the girl's ear, and her brother was helping so the child would not be afraid, Peter and his helpers set the bread and milk on the table. There was nothing with which to squeeze orange juice, so Peter cut some of the fruit in half and said the children could eat them with spoons.

Doctor Wood put something in Tootsy's ear that stopped the pain at once, and he promised to send some medicine for her to take so that the ear-ache would not come back. She stopped crying, and began to eat bread and milk as soon as she was seated at the table.

"I'll take Honey Bunch and Ida and Grace home," offered the good doctor when he saw Peter Noble look at his watch. "I suppose you're due on duty."

The policeman said he was, and hurried away after telling the Nock children he would look in again to see how they were. Doctor Wood promised Willie he would take him to the hospital to see his mother as soon as she was well enough to receive visitors. Then he and his three "passengers" said good-bye and went down to his car.

The doctor had a call to make, so he dropped Honey Bunch at her house without going in himself. He let Ida and Grace out at Grace's house, for Ida meant to see that Grace put the pearl beads in a box as a present for Ruth Noble's wedding.

When Honey Bunch opened the door of her house she was surprised to find three suitcases in the hall. Then she heard familiar voices, and rushed into the living room to find her own dear mother and daddy talking to Mrs. Miller. There was a little girl, too, who rushed at her, tripping over a rug as she came. Throwing her arms around Honey Bunch, she cried, "Oh, I thought you never would come back to your house today. Where have you been?"

This was Stub Morton, a cousin who lived

on a farm and who was always an interesting visitor because one never knew what she might do next. Before Honey Bunch could as much as kiss her mother and daddy, Stub had explained that "Aunt Edith," who was Honey Bunch's mother, had stopped at the farm for one day and had brought Stub back with her for a visit.

"We met Uncle David at the Junction and he said 'Good gracious' when he saw me," confessed Stub. "Uncle David" was Honey Bunch's daddy.

"Stub, dear, if you'll keep still just a minute I'd like to hear what Mrs. Miller has to tell me," suggested Mrs. Morton gently.

"Well, I guess I've told you most everything," the laundress said. "The wash has disappeared. There's a young, good-looking policeman supposed to be following it up, but I can't see that he does much about it. I never was so upset in my life—it's the first time I was ever left to keep house and couldn't turn things back just as good as I found them. The clothes-basket's gone, too."

"Oh, but we've found it!" Honey Bunch could keep still no longer. "We found the wash and the clothes-basket and Peter Noble knows all about it. The Nock children's mother is in the hospital and Mrs. Denty told them they could wear my clothes. Doctor Wood is curing Tootsy Nock's ear-ache. It's all right, Mother, we found the wash."

Mr. and Mrs. Morton stared at their daughter in amazement. Mrs. Miller fanned herself with a newspaper as if she felt faint. And Stub for once in her life did not have a word to say.

"Where *have* you been, Honey Bunch?" gasped her mother. "What *are* you talking about? Who are all these strange people you mention? I never heard their names before."

"Begin at the beginning, Honey Bunch," her daddy encouraged her. "Tell us slowly what has happened and then we'll understand."

Honey Bunch then gave her story and they all listened to her as if they were afraid to miss a word.

When she had finished, her mother said, "Oh, David, those poor, forlorn children!"

Her daddy added, "I think we'll have to do something about this."

"I hope you get the wash back right away so I can fumigate it," declared Mrs. Miller. "Goodness only knows what kind of a place it is where those youngsters live."

"I have an idea that family needs the things more than we do," Mr. Morton answered. "I've about made up my mind to let them keep whatever will be of use to them. I can get Honey Bunch some new frocks and her mother some new towels. We'll take back the table linen with our initials, but the sheets will be useful to that family when the mother is brought back from the hospital. Yes, I think we'll have to let the Nock family have the wash. But suppose we go and see them first, Edith?"

Honey Bunch's pretty mother had been traveling since early that morning, but she stood up and put on her hat at once.

"Let's go now, dear," she suggested. "I can't rest until I know those children are properly provided for. Bring the car around and we'll drive over right away."

Honey Bunch was left to entertain Stub. They were on their way to the playroom when the telephone rang. Honey Bunch answered it and Stub sat down on the stairs to wait for her.

"Why, Ruth!" cried Honey Bunch. "Yes, I knew you. Oh, what happened? Is she very sick? Is she sorry? You want me? Oh, I think that's lovely! Nothing like that ever happened to me. Yes, of course I can. Yes, my mother's home. I'll tell her. Good-bye."

Stub complained that she could not understand what the people on the phone were talking about.

"It sounds so silly," she declared, "when you can't hear what the other person is saying."

"You come on upstairs and I'll tell you," said Honey Bunch. "It's a secret, that is, a kind of a secret. I can tell you and my mother and Ida and Grace and maybe Norman. But it isn't the kind of secret you tell everyone."

Stub bounded up the steps after Honey Bunch, and when they were in the playroom she shut the door with a bang.

"Now tell me!" she begged. "Tell me, quick. I love secrets."

CHAPTER XIII

A MISSING MESSENGER BOY

"THAT was Ruth Noble who called up," explained Honey Bunch.

Naturally Stub said, "Who's Ruth Noble?" and Honey Bunch had to tell her cousin about the policeman's sister, and that she was to be married Saturday.

"She invited Ida and Grace and me to the wedding," confided Honey Bunch, "though she isn't going to have any feathers. And now, what do you think?"

"Why isn't she going to have any feathers?" Stub demanded. She was interested, and wanted to know all the reasons for everything.

"Well, Fred said they weren't going to have any fuss or feathers," explained little Honey Bunch. "I think that means Ruth won't wear a train and a veil. Fred is her fiance," she added hastily, seeing another question forming on Stub's lips. "A fiance is the man a girl marries. His name is Fred Paull, and he's nice."

"All right," said Stub, satisfied. "Go on."

"Ruth called up to tell me that her cousin who was to be flower girl has the measles," Honey Bunch obediently "went on," trying not to stare at a large spot on the front of Stub's dress. "Ruth said she isn't going to have bridesmaids, but she wanted her cousin to hold her flowers during the—the wedding. Now, the cousin's sick and can't, and she has asked me if I should like to be her flower girl!"

"Oh, gee, that's great!" approved Stub. "You'll be a nice flower girl, Honey Bunch. You won't drop anything or fall over anything. And you'll be right up front where you can hear everything the minister says."

"I'll ask if you can come, too," Honey Bunch promised. "And I'll tell you what we're going to give Ruth for a wedding present—a string of pearl beads. Come on over to Grace's house now and I'll show them to you."

They left word with Mrs. Miller where they were going. Out on the front steps they found Norman Clark who promptly announced that he was going, too.

"Where were you after lunch, Honey Bunch?" he asked, falling into step beside her. "I looked all over for you after I got home."

His playmate explained what had happened, and Stub was even more interested than Norman because each time she heard about the stolen wash she learned more about the old trunk and pearl beads and Carter Street, and the mystery was delightfully jumbled in her mind.

"Your dress is kind of spotty to go to see people in," said Honey Bunch mildly, as they reached Grace's house.

"Yes, I know, but my suitcase isn't unpacked," Stub apologized. "I spilled ice cream soda on the front of this."

Ida and Grace were upstairs in Grace's room, Mrs. Winters said smilingly. She told the visitors to "go right up." They found their friends admiring the pearl beads which they had arranged on some clean pink cotton in a pretty gray box.

"It looks just like a wedding present,

doesn't it?" said Honey Bunch happily. "Now we will have to send it to Ruth. Shall we mail it?"

No one had any money for postage, and Grace objected that they did not know where Ruth Noble lived.

"We can look it up in the phone book," suggested Ida. "Why can't Norman take it to her? You'll be careful, won't you, Norman?"

The idea of acting as delivery boy pleased Norman and made him feel very important. He clattered downstairs and looked up the Nobles' address in the telephone book, then clattered up again to get the package.

"Print on it 'From your friends', Norman, please," said Honey Bunch. "You print such nice letters."

The boy did as she asked, then slipped the box inside his pocket and was ready to start.

"Be sure to come back here and tell us what she said, Norman," Grace directed. "We'll wait for you. Don't go in and stay—that isn't polite."

The little lad set off at a speed that indicated he might arrive at Ruth Noble's without any breath left in his body, and the four little girls crowded into the window seat to wait for him. While they sat there, Honey Bunch told Ida and Grace what her daddy had decided to do about the wash.

"Daddy and Mother are over there now," she said, "and Mrs. Miller said Mother told her that Tootsy could have some more of my clothes if she needs them."

"I guess the Nock family will be all right after this," Ida remarked with satisfaction. "Your father and mother will be nice to them and Doctor Wood will cure Tootsy. Then Peter will help Willie. I heard him tell Willie he could get him a job for Saturdays, perhaps."

"Say, I think Norman is taking his own time," Grace complained. "Let's walk down to meet him. He might go home and never tell us a thing."

The four went all the way to the Noble house without meeting Norman. Grace was sure he had gone home, but Honey Bunch declared that their messenger boy would not do that.

"He said he'd come back to your house,

Grace, and I'm sure he would," she insisted. "He must be inside, talking to Ruth."

The girls looked at the Noble house. It was a little place, but very neat, with dainty curtains at all the windows. There was no porch, just a white-painted door set in the red brick wall. A knocker of brass winked at them brightly.

"Shall we go in and ask if he's here?" whispered Grace, as if the people in the house might hear her.

"I think we'd better not," Ida objected, for she was timid.

"It won't hurt to ask if he's been here," decided Honey Bunch. "We won't go inside. We'll just say, 'Is Norman Clark here?' Or, 'Has a boy named Norman Clark been here?' "

Honey Bunch lifted the knocker, and they could hear footsteps coming to the door. It opened, and Peter Noble stood looking down at them.

"Well, more callers!" he exclaimed. "Come in, won't you? My mother and sister are out, but there's a friend of yours here."

The children stepped over the door-sill directly into a pleasant living room. There was no hall. Over by a side window they saw Norman Clark, who looked surprised to see them.

"She wasn't home, but she'll be back any minute," he began to explain right away. "I thought I'd better wait."

"Stub, this is Peter Noble," said Honey Bunch politely, remembering that the two had never met. "Peter, this is my cousin Stub."

"How do you do, and where's your uniform?" inquired Stub, staring critically at the tall young man.

"I'm not wearing it much this week," he told her. "I'm on what we call plainclothes duty. We go without our uniforms and wear ordinary clothes so that people will not know we are policemen."

Peter found chairs for all of them, explaining that he and Norman had been talking about Jake Silberman, the second-hand man.

"He wasn't arrested, Honey Bunch," Norman assured her. "Peter had a clue about the attic things. You remember, the things that were stolen from his mother's attic."

"Yes," said Peter. "I had a clue. I've never

given up hope of finding those things which mean so much to my mother. The clue led me to Silberman's, but I didn't get very far there."

Honey Bunch resolved to ask the other members of the Detective Club if they did not think it would be nice to offer to follow clues for Peter. Now that they had found the wash, the Club was really out of work. Perhaps if they put their heads together they could find the missing "attic things" for Peter's mother. However, Honey Bunch could not very well suggest this to the man, until she had asked the others if they were willing to help.

"Did you look around Jake's yard?" asked Norman. He had been talking for half an hour to Peter, and felt just like a policeman himself.

"It wouldn't do any good to look around that mess for things which were stolen years ago," the man said, smiling. "No, I told Silberman what I knew, and he promised to search and bring me word. I haven't much hope, but as I say, I don't like to give up. My mother would be so happy to have this mystery solved, though."

The door opened suddenly and in walked Ruth Noble and her mother. Mrs. Noble was tall like Peter, and smiling and slim. She had white hair, but she did not look a bit like an old lady. She said she was very glad to meet so many nice friends of Peter and Ruth, and would they please stay to tea?

"No-o, thank you, we can't do that," Honey Bunch answered, as the others lapsed into silence. "We just wanted to see Ruth a minute."

"Mother, may Hunter come in?" asked Peter. "The children would like to see him."

Mrs. Noble laughed a little as she explained that she always put the dog in the garden when she went out. "For if Peter goes off and leaves him in the house, the rooms will be wrecked before I get home," she said.

She went out to the kitchen and in a few moments Hunter bounded in. He was delighted to see his master, pleased to greet Ruth, and was as happy as could be to find five children waiting for him. He barked, and choked, and choked, and barked, and had a grand time before he finally consented to lie down on the rug and keep quiet.

"We brought you a present," said Honey Bunch to Ruth a little shyly. "Norman has it in his pocket."

"You brought me a present?" Ruth Noble cried. "Why, how lovely! Peter, aren't they sweet to bring me a present?"

She looked so pretty, so radiantly happy, so sparkling and gay, that all the children looked at her and smiled. Norman pulled the box from his pocket and placed it on her lap. Then they all watched eagerly as she opened the package.

"'From your friends,'" she read aloud. "Oh, this is exciting. Only you shouldn't bring me a present. I told you there was to be no fuss nor feathers."

She unloosened the string and was just taking off the piece of wrapping paper, when Hunter began to bark furiously.

"Someone at the door, Peter," said Ruth, glancing over her shoulder.

Her brother strode to the door and flung it open. On the step stood the bearded second-hand man, Jake Silberman.

CHAPTER XIV

A GREAT SURPRISE

"WHY, come in, Jake," said Peter Noble.

The second-hand man peered into the room and shook his head.

"I see you got company—I won't bother you," he mumbled. "But about that trunk, Mr. Noble. I got some information, I think."

"Come in, come in," the policeman urged. "These are some young friends of ours. Come in and tell me what you've found out."

Jake Silberman sidled into the living room, but did not look very comfortable. Kind Ruth Noble knew what the matter was with him—he was embarrassed to find himself among so many people.

"I'm sure you wish to speak to my brother alone, Mr. Silberman," said Ruth pleasantly. "The rest of us will go upstairs. You'd like to see my wedding gifts, wouldn't you, girls?"

Indeed they would, and said so. Ruth asked

Norman if he did not want to go with them, but the boy thought that wedding presents were only for girls to look at.

"I'll stay with the men," he said grandly, trying to lean back in his chair as Peter Noble did. Only the chair was so deep and Norman was such a small lad that he fell back almost as if he were going into a hole.

Ruth Noble led the way upstairs to a front room where her gifts were on display. She had everything arranged very nicely, and for a girl who did not intend to have any "fuss or feathers" at her wedding, she certainly had a good many beautiful presents.

"This is my linen," she explained, pointing to a large cedar chest filled with towels and tablecloths, sheets and pillow cases. "Peter and my mother gave me the linen and Fred gave me the chest."

She showed the wide-eyed Honey Bunch and the other girls how she had all these things tied up with embroidered bands, and then explained that in her new home Fred Paull had built her a closet with each shelf edged with a cretonne ruffle.

"You must come and see me in my own

house," said Ruth, smiling. "Mother says it's like a doll's. Perhaps I'll give a tea party and you can all bring your dolls."

Stub was not much interested in linens, but she admired all the shiny knives and forks and spoons—six drawers filled with them—all placed in neat rows.

"Fred's office friends gave us that," Ruth explained. "Fred made Peter promise to come over once a week and help us polish the silver."

"That's a lovely tea set," murmured Honey Bunch, pointing to a table which held half a dozen pink cups and saucers. The cups were banded in silver and were very beautiful.

"Oh, that's one of my most treasured presents," said Ruth, her eyes shining. "My darling Aunt Vera sent it to me from England. I have the tea pot and the cake plate packed, but I left the cups out to show them to people."

"Ruth! Ruth! Are you busy?" called someone.

"That's Peter," Ruth announced. "He must want me and I'll have to go down. You stay here till I come back. Look at everything as much as you please, but I'd rather you didn't touch anything."

"You haven't opened our present yet, you know," Honey Bunch reminded her.

"Good gracious, so I didn't!" cried Ruth. "I put it on top of my little new radio, didn't I? Well, that just shows how getting married affects me. I forget everything. This is the first time I have been married, you know, so I don't know how to act."

"Ruth!" called Peter again, and this time it sounded as if he might be impatient.

"Darlings, I'll have to go and see what that brother of mine wants," the young woman apologized. "I'll hurry back and open my present. Don't let anyone open it for me. I'm so eager to see what's inside that box."

She darted out of the room, and the children heard her little sharp heels go tap-tap-tap down the stairs.

"I think she's lovely!" said Ida. "And she has splendid wedding presents. It must be fun to get married and have people send you things."

"I'd like a tool-chest," Stub declared.

"Would anyone send me a tool-chest if I got married?"

"That isn't a lady-present," objected Grace Winters. "I never heard of anyone getting a tool-chest for a wedding present."

Stub said if she could not have a tool-chest she would not get married, and Honey Bunch said she thought a tea set was much nicer than a tool-chest.

"A tea set!" Stub remarked in scorn. "Ho, anybody can have a tea set. Why, I wouldn't care if I never had a tea set."

She flung out her arm to show how little she cared for tea sets and almost lost her balance. She caught herself in time, but her foot tangled in the rug and she lurched against the table. Over it went, and the lovely pink and silver tea cups went crashing to the floor.

"Oh, Stub, Stub!" wailed Honey Bunch. "They're broken! Stub, those cups are broken, and they're wedding present cups!"

Stub was down on the floor, mournfully trying to gather up the pieces.

"I didn't mean to knock 'em over," she wept. "I didn't mean to break a single thing.

Maybe my mother can buy some more cups."

Ida shook her head, the tears rolling down her cheeks.

"Nobody can buy any more cups," she choked. "Don't you remember Ruth said they came from England? Her aunt sent them to her."

There was a little noise at the door and Ruth herself came into the room.

"I thought I heard something," she began. Then she saw the overturned table. "Oh, my cups!" She darted forward. "Why, they're broken! What happened?"

Stub was so blinded by tears that she could not see where she was going. She got to her feet and would have walked into another table on which was placed the new radio, if Ruth had not stopped her.

"It's all my fault!" wept Honey Bunch's cousin. "I do everything wrong. Everything! I knocked the table over and your wedding is all spoiled and my mother can't buy you cups like these because they came from England. I am so sorry," choked poor Stub. "I am so sorry I feel dreadful inside of me!"

Ruth Noble patted the little girl's shoulder

without saying anything for a moment. Honey Bunch, when she saw how sadly Ruth looked at the pieces of broken china, felt "dreadful inside," too. Yet when Ruth did speak, her voice was, as usual, gentle and kind.

"It was an accident, Stub, I know," said Ruth. "I can't say it doesn't matter, because it does matter very much to me. My Aunt Vera is my favorite aunt and anything she sends me I love for her own sake. But when an accident happens it doesn't help anyone to fuss about it or to be too unhappy. So we won't say any more about this. Let me sweep up the china, though, before any of you children cut yourselves on the sharp edges."

The young woman brought a pan and a soft brush and cleared away the broken pieces. Then she took up the package she had put on the radio.

"Now, chickens, don't look so glum," she commanded. "We're going to think of happy things. Of what's in this box, for instance. You all know, but I don't. It isn't heavy. I wonder what it can be."

She sat down in a low chair. Honey Bunch,

"OH, HOW PRETTY!" SHE CRIED SOFTLY. "I NEVER SAW SUCH PRETTY PEARL BEADS."

Ida, Grace and Stub gathered around her. They forgot the broken cups as they watched Ruth take off the wrapping paper and lift the lid of the box. She took up the string of pearl beads and held them to the light.

"Oh, how pretty!" she cried softly, her face flushing with pleasure. "I never saw such pretty pearl beads. Never! I'll have to wear them on my wedding day."

She dropped the beads into her lap and leaned forward.

"Thank you, Honey Bunch!" she cried prettily, kissing her. "Thank you, Ida! Thank you, Grace! Thank you, Stub!" And she kissed each little girl in turn.

"I didn't have anything to do with the present," said the honest Stub. "I just came with Honey Bunch. The other girls thought it all up."

Ruth said she was sure Stub *would* have had something to do with the pearl beads if she had lived in Barham as the others did, and then and there she invited the visitor to come to her wedding.

Downstairs the front door slammed, meaning that Jake Silberman had gone, Ruth announced. A moment later Peter Noble and Norman strolled into the room, both pretending that they were not interested in wedding presents, but had just come up to learn "what there was to see," as the patrolman expressed it.

"Well, Peter, perhaps you'll be good enough to give us your opinion of my wedding present," said his sister gaily. "Look what these blessed children have brought me! Isn't it lovely?"

Her brother took the necklace and turned it over in his hands.

"I think I'll wear them at my wedding," Ruth informed him happily.

Peter said nothing, but continued to gaze at the beads.

"I told the girls I'd never seen any half so pretty," went on his sister. "Mother will love them, too. Why don't you say something, Peter? Don't you like my beautiful present?"

For answer the young policeman walked swiftly to the door and closed it. Then he came back to the astonished group, and his voice, when he did speak, was harsh and stern.

"Look here, where did these come from?"

he asked, letting the string of beads dangle from his finger. "Have you children been up to anything you shouldn't? You surely haven't helped yourself to your mother's jewels or to a neighbor's, have you, in order to give my sister a remembrance?"

The girls and Norman stared at him, frightened more by his voice and the look on his face than by what he said. They did not know what he was talking about. Neither did his pretty sister.

"Peter!" Ruth protested. "Peter, how can you be so brutal? Why should you talk like that to these youngsters?"

Her brother looked directly at Honey Bunch as he replied.

"I talk like this because it's necessary," he said grimly. "These are very, very valuable pearls. Pearls, mind you."

Honey Bunch looked at the beads which she rather expected to see changed into something else. But they appeared to be the same as she had always seen them.

"Do you mean they're *real* pearls?" she heard Ruth gasp.

"A matched strand," Peter said in that

strange, hard voice. "I may be unduly suspicious, but I never before heard of children handing out matched pearls as a wedding gift."

Ruth said "Oh!" in a very small voice.

Norman tried to squeeze himself behind a chair and Ida and Grace looked ready to cry. Only Stub didn't seem to mind. She just stared, for she had had nothing to do with these beads.

"Now one of you had better speak up and tell me exactly how you got hold of these pearls," said Peter Noble firmly. "The thing to do is to go back to the beginning and remember everything you can. *Where did you get these pearls?*"

"I—I thought they were just beads," murmured Honey Bunch, seeing that none of the others were likely to "speak up" or help her out. "I found them."

"Where?" Peter demanded.

"In the trunk," said Honey Bunch. "It was after the wash was stolen. We had a detective club and went down to Jake Silberman's to follow a clue."

"I see." Peter's voice sounded more kind. "Who went with you, Honey Bunch?"

"Ida and Grace did," answered Honey Bunch. "But after we got there we found Norman in a trunk. When we were pulling him out the paper lining tore and I found the pearl beads, I mean the pearls."

"Were they in this box?" Peter pointed to the box Ruth held on her lap.

"No, they were in a paper," replied Honey Bunch. "Mr. Silberman chased us when we were trying to read the writing, and——"

"Writing?" almost shouted Peter. "Did you say there was writing on this paper? What did it say? Who wrote it?"

"Now, Peter, don't frighten the child," Ruth said gently. "She's telling you everything you want to know and it isn't fair to shout at her."

Her brother smiled at Honey Bunch.

"Excuse my policeman manners," he apologized. "I don't mean to be impolite. Just tell me, in your own way, what the writing was on this paper. What it said, I mean."

Honey Bunch wrinkled her brows.

"Well, I can't remember just what it said," she confided.

"Was it a letter, dear?" asked Ruth.

"No, not a letter."

"Was it written in pencil or in ink?" Peter asked.

"In ink."

"Now, think a moment," advised Ruth. "Don't try to hurry your thoughts. Do you remember how the paper looked, Honey Bunch? Perhaps the words will come back to you."

It was all very well for them to tell her to think, the little girl said to herself, but she could not think because she kept wondering what made Peter and Ruth Noble seem so excited. The young woman's cheeks were burning red and her eyes were shining. Peter kept walking up and down and looked as upset as his sister did. All this excitement over a piece of paper with writing on it puzzled Honey Bunch. The beads, no, the pearls, were more important than that faded ink, she thought.

"I can't remember what the writing was," she confessed reluctantly.

"Oh, Honey Bunch!" cried Ruth in evident dismay.

Peter came up to Honey Bunch and towered over her.

"You *must* think!" he commanded. "I must know everything! Do you hear me, Honey Bunch? Everything depends upon it. Think!"

CHAPTER XV

A HAPPY ENDING

IDA was a shy little girl, but a very loyal friend. She wanted so much to help Honey Bunch that she made herself speak.

"Honey Bunch!" she said clearly, "Honey Bunch, don't you remember what you said? You thought it was a birthday. Someone sent it on a birthday, you said."

Ruth cried "Oh!" very softly, and Peter took a short walk up and down the room.

"I wish you could recall it, Honey Bunch," he groaned.

"I do!" Honey Bunch cried suddenly, opening her blue eyes wide. "I do remember. Ida made me. And walking up and down doesn't help me at all."

Peter Noble laughed a little and stopped his tramping.

"What do you remember, Honey Bunch?" he begged respectfully. "You'll tell us, won't you?"

"Yes," Honey Bunch nodded. "Let me think a minute."

She closed her eyes and tried to see the paper as it had looked.

"It said 'To my dear granddaughter Fanny. Each pearl is for many happy hours to come,' " recited Honey Bunch.

"Did you hear that, Peter?" cried Ruth in great excitement. "Did you hear what Honey Bunch said? I must call Mother!"

Her brother shook his head.

"Don't let's stir up Mother over this, Sis," he urged, "until we really know all about it. Her mind's full of your wedding now and a lot of extra excitement might be too much for her. Better wait."

Ruth murmured that perhaps he was right, but she looked rather disappointed.

Honey Bunch had been thinking hard. She knew about the old trunk, of course. And about the pearl "beads" and the paper in which they had been wrapped. But she remembered something else, too. What was it Peter Noble had told her and Mrs. Miller, when he had come to ask more questions about the stolen wash? Honey Bunch recalled how he had looked, with his high boots and his slicker over his uniform.

"Why, Peter, you told us about your great-grandmother's things!" cried Honey Bunch. "When Hunter chased Lady Clare—remember? But you didn't say a word about a trunk, did you? Were the cables and the lace and the books in a trunk? And were the pearls your great-grandmother's pearls?"

"Sables, Honey Bunch, not cables," Peter corrected, laughing, and Ruth had to laugh, too. "Sables are furs, dear. Yes, all these valuables were stored in an old trunk, and you seem to have found that very trunk. But we won't speak of it to my mother just yet. I must see Silberman."

The policeman looked at his watch. It was six o'clock, which was dinner time for most people.

"I'll have to run these children home in the car, Ruth," said Peter. "Their families will begin to worry about them. I'll stop in at Honey Bunch's house and have a look at that paper. Tell Mother I'll be back in half an hour."

Norman, who had been still even longer than Honey Bunch had ever known him to be, recovered his speech in the car. He wanted to go in with the policeman and Honey Bunch and help them look at the paper. Ida and Grace would have liked to have been there too, but they did not say so.

"Well, Norman, if it's all the same to you," Peter Noble announced cheerfully, "I'd rather talk to Mr. and Mrs. Morton without an audience. I'm much obliged to you, however, for crawling into the trunk and getting stuck there. Otherwise my great-grandmother's pearls might never have been found."

"But now we haven't any wedding present for Ruth!" said Honey Bunch sadly.

"Goodness, what do you call a string of matched pearls?" Peter asked her. "She would never have had them if it hadn't been for you. And there is no wedding present that will mean as much to her. I only hope she doesn't think more of her pearls than she does of her husband!"

He set Ida down at her house and Grace at hers, and then drove to Honey Bunch's home.

Norman's daddy was waiting on the front steps to tell his son to come right home to dinner, so that settled the boy.

Mr. and Mrs. Morton were surprised to see Peter come in with their little daughter and Stub, but of course they had heard all about him from Mrs. Miller. Honey Bunch ran up to the playroom and brought down the box which held the precious paper. He read it very carefully, as if he were afraid it might dissolve into thin air. "To my dear granddaughter Fanny. Each pearl is for many happy years to come."

"There's no use going to that junk yard tonight, Mr. Noble," Honey Bunch's daddy pointed out. "It will be too dark to see your way around. If the trunk is still there it will keep till morning."

The policeman said yes, he supposed so. He looked at Honey Bunch and smiled.

"Since you and Norman really found the pearls, I think you ought to help me follow the last clue," he said. The little girl had told him about the Detective Club. "I'll call for you at eight o'clock in the morning."

You may be sure that Honey Bunch was up

long before breakfast the next day. Stub overslept and Mrs. Morton said not to call her, for she could not go to the junk yard anyway. Peter could not take so many in his car.

Honey Bunch had told Norman before his bedtime the night before about the invitation and he came over and had breakfast with her. "So as not to be late," he told the exasperated Mrs. Miller.

Daddy Morton was to go with them, and three minutes before eight o'clock found the four tucked into Peter Noble's auto. He wore his uniform this morning and looked very imposing.

Jake Silberman thought so, too. Honey Bunch could see that he was very much in awe of that policeman's blue suit.

"Jake, I want to look at that trunk in your yard, the one these children were playing in," said Peter soberly. "We're pretty sure it is the one that was stolen from my mother's attic. I saw it a hundred times when I was a kid, and think I'll recognize it."

The trunk was exactly as Honey Bunch had last seen it. Peter went over it thoroughly, nodding his head as if satisfied.

"That's the one," he declared. "See, if you look closely you'll find my great-grandmother's initials, 'F.D.A.', showing faintly under this handle. Her name was Frances Derry Acton."

"I'm glad you found it, Mr. Noble," said the second-hand dealer, his stubby gray beard wagging as he talked. "But there's nothing in the trunk. As a matter of fact, I bought it empty. Thought I could sell it to somebody cheap.

"I have located that old book I told you about, the one in which I put down the sales for the year I bought this old trunk. If you'll come up to the house, I'll show it to you."

Everyone followed the short, stout figure to the house, where Mrs. Silberman dusted off chairs with her apron and brought a fat, greasy-looking book from the big safe under the windows in the front room. Honey Bunch did not want to touch such a dirty object and Norman could not get near enough to see the pages.

Peter Noble and Honey Bunch's daddy were very much interested. They turned over page after page, and the junk man tried to help them, until at last the policeman cried in an excited voice, "Here it is!"

He then read aloud: "Paid Ada Horn $10 for empty trunk, June 11, 1920." He now looked at the second-hand dealer and almost shouted, "Jake, Ada Horn was a maid employed by my mother. She left us in a huff. But I remember my mother worrying because she had a pass-key to the house. It was six months later the trunk was stolen, so Ada must have let herself in with the key when we were all away. No one saw her, and even if anyone did, he might have thought she had come back to work for us. She took that trunk, all right."

"Where," said Honey Bunch eagerly, "are the cables? And the books, and the pictures, and things?"

"The *sables* are gone and so's everything, I'm afraid, except the most valuable of all the heirlooms, the pearls," Peter replied.

"Oh, there's a fan!" cried Norman. "Jake gave it to Honey Bunch. And I have a knife. Did your mother have a knife in the trunk?"

Peter laughed and said he thought not. He told Honey Bunch to keep the little fan as a memento of her first mystery.

"Only the missing wash was the real mystery, wasn't it?" Peter asked. "If Willie and Tootsy Nock had not taken your mother's clothes, my mother might never have learned what happened to her missing trunk."

Everyone thought this was true and the children were almost glad it happened.

"Isn't it funny how you start one place and end up in another?" laughed Honey Bunch. She was right and was going to think of this on her next adventure, "Her First Little Circus."

"Don't forget that we have a wedding in our family tomorrow," Peter reminded Honey Bunch as they drove back to the Morton house. "Ruth tells me you're to be the flower girl. The flower girl, you know, has to keep the best man from crying," he added, laughing.

But no one cried at the wedding the next day. Honey Bunch wore her best blue silk dress that matched her blue eyes. Ruth looked lovely in a blue suit with a pretty hat, the brim of which was faced with a shade to match the larkspurs she carried. While she was being married, Honey Bunch, standing very straight, held the armful of beautiful flowers.

The church was filled with guests, though no invitations had been issued. But all the people who knew Ruth loved her and wanted to see her married, so they came to church just as they would have on a Sunday morning. Stub, Ida, Grace and Norman sat in one of the front pews with Mrs. Morton, whom Ruth had asked to come, too. In another seat was Mrs. Noble, looking very happy indeed. Peter was best man, and though he was plainly trying to be good in church, he looked much more likely to laugh than to cry. As for Fred Paull, "the fiance," as Honey Bunch insisted on calling him, he had no eyes for anyone but his lovely Ruth.

After the ceremony a few people were expected at the Noble house for a small reception. Honey Bunch very proudly rode with the bridal party in Peter's car. Fred Paull's cousin, Dick Rogers, drove Mrs. Morton and Stub, Ida and Grace in his car.

"Did you wear the pearls, Ruth?" cried Grace, as soon as she was in the house. "We couldn't see from where we sat. Stub said you didn't have them on."

"The lady you are addressing is Mrs. Frederic T. Paull," Peter informed the little girl with a grand air that made them all laugh.

"I'll always be the same old Ruth to my friends," declared the pretty bride, blushing a becoming rosy red. "Certainly I am wearing my lovely pearls, Grace. See?"

She took off her light fur scarf and the beautiful creamy pearls showed up, a circlet around her throat.

"I think Honey Bunch should have the first slice of wedding cake!" said the white-haired Mrs. Noble. "She found the pearls and saved the paper dear Grandmother Acton gave with them. I think that means as much to me as the pearls mean to Ruth."

So, in the dining room, when the beautiful white cake was cut, the first piece went to Honey Bunch.

"You take it home and put it under your pillow and you will have a dream, Honey

Bunch," whispered Stub. "Mrs. Miller told me that this morning."

"You eat six slices and you'll have a wonder dream, Honey Bunch," Fred Paull called across the table.

"I'm going to save my cake," announced Honey Bunch seriously, "to remember the wedding day."

"And what will you remember me by, darling?" the bride asked, with her lovely smile.

Honey Bunch thought a moment.

"By the feathers," she explained, "that you didn't have at your wedding."

THE END

[illegible]

"And what will you remember me by, darling?" [illegible] her lovely smile.

Henry Smith thought a moment.

"By the feathers," she explained. "That you didn't have at your wedding!"

THE END